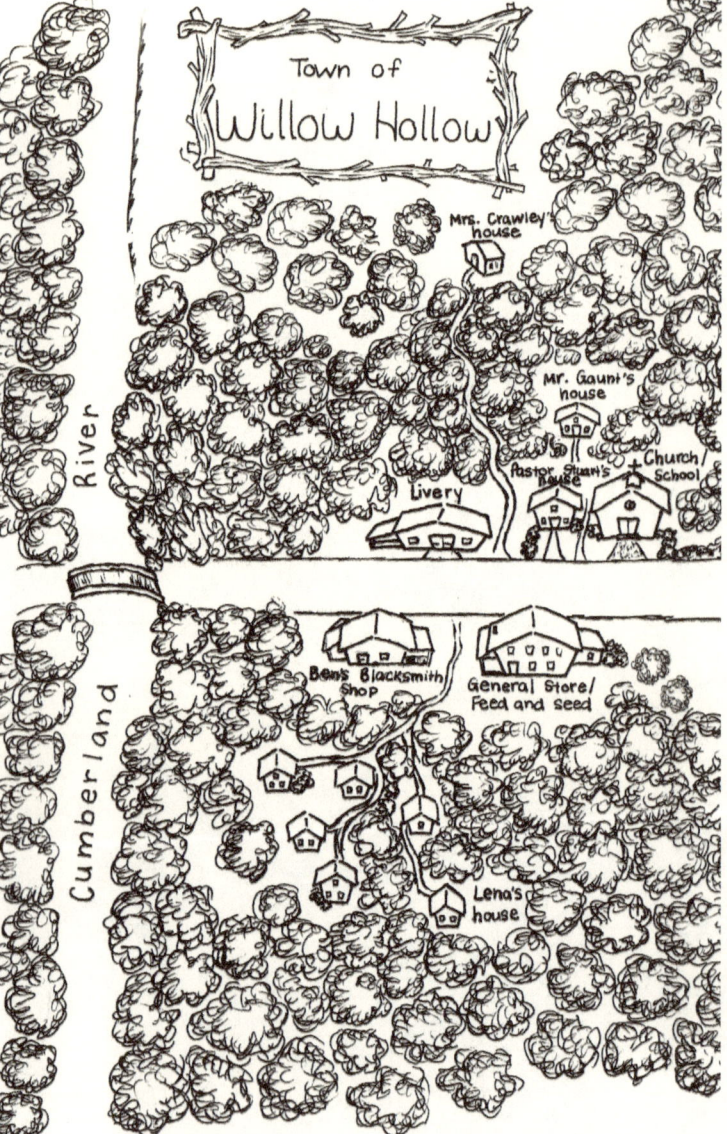

Town of
Willow Hollow

River

Mrs. Crawley's house

Mr. Gaunt's house

Pastor Stuart's house

Church/School

Livery

Cumberland

Ben's Blacksmith Shop

General Store/Feed and seed

Lena's house

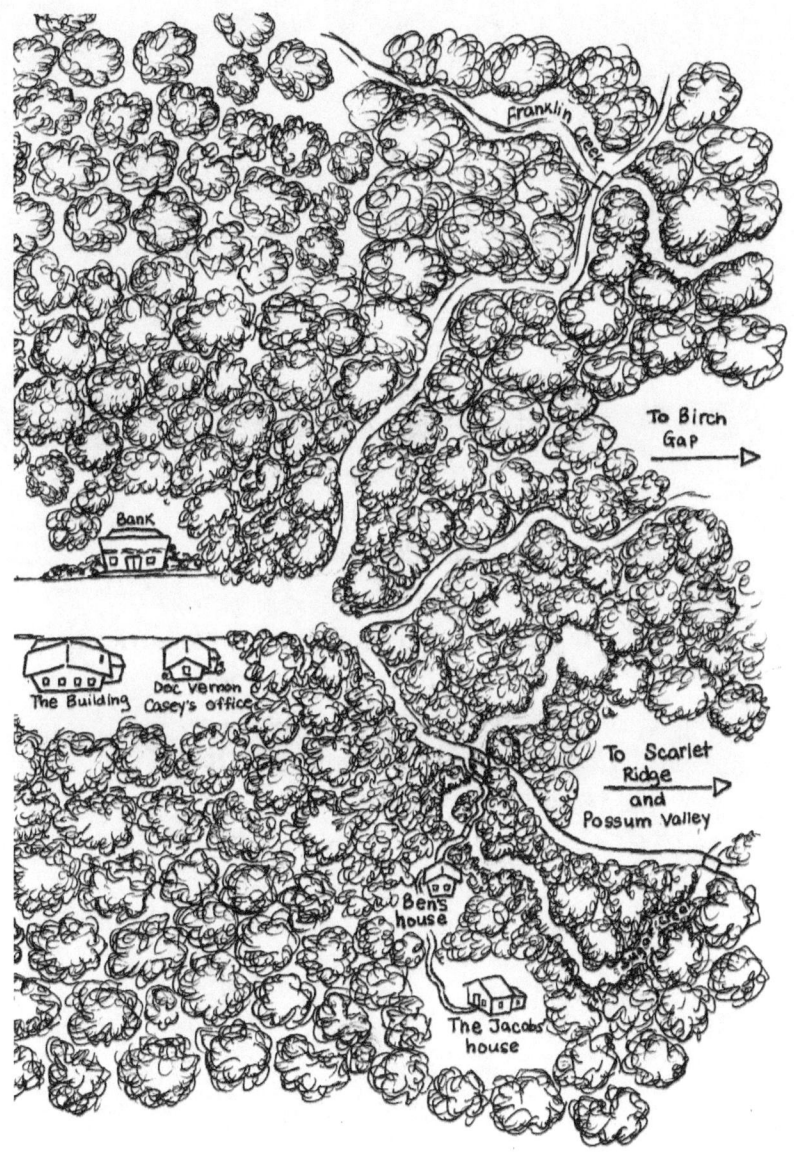

Franklin

To Birch
Gap

Bank

The Building

Doc Vernon
Casey's office

To Scarlet
Ridge
and
Possum Valley

Ben's
house

The Jacobs
house

A Strand of Hope

A *Strand* of *Hope*

Amanda Tero

A Strand of Hope

© 2020 by Amanda Tero

Published by Amanda Tero
Decatur, MS 39327

All Scripture references taken from the King James Version. Public domain.

This novella is a work of fiction. The characters in this story are fictitious. Any resemblance to persons living or dead is coincidental.

ISBN: 978-1-942931-32-4

_____

Cover design by Amanda Tero
Images from
   www.pixabay.com
   www.shutterstock.com
Used by permission.

Willow Hollow map copyright 2020 by Elisabeth Grothjan,
   SparrowandRoseDesigns@gmail.com
Used by permission.

Formatted by Amanda Tero

For my sister, Elizabeth

This book is all your fault—not that
I'm complaining. Thanks for sharing
that random Packhorse Librarian video
on my Facebook timeline and putting
another project on my plate. But more
than that, thanks for being my sister
through thick and thin, and for
balancing me out all these years.
Love you bunches!

1

Saturday, January 25, 1936

The muffled sound of dishes crashing in the kitchen jerked Lena's focus away from her book. She crouched lower and brought the pages closer to her face, hiding in the folds of her coat and blanket. Folks were saying that Kentucky was experiencing an unusually cold winter. Last weekend, she wouldn't have believed them, but this weekend, she had to agree. It was too cold to be out here, really. But it was better out here half freezing than in there with Mom.

The screen door popped open then snapped against the door frame as it slammed shut.

"Lena!"

There it was.

Lena glanced at the bottom of the book. Page 92. She had read Gaskell's *North and South* three times, but it didn't matter. She didn't want to abandon Margaret Hale as she was leaving sick Bessy in her suffering. The oppression Margaret felt seeped into Lena's soul. Bessy was as much Lena's friend as she was Margaret's in the story.

"Leeena!"

Lena swallowed. It wasn't her full name yet, but impatience was etched in Mom's tone. Lena wrapped the blanket tighter around her and stood as a wave of chills swept over her—hiding the book in the folds of the tattered quilt as she turned to face Mom.

The stoop to Mom's shoulders and the way she shaded her eyes even though the sun's glare wasn't *that* bright sealed Lena's suspicions. Mom had come home drunk again last night and had spent the day sleeping it off.

"Yes ma'am?" Lena tried to swallow her irritation, but the glassy look Mom gave her revealed she hadn't tried hard enough.

"Why aren't the dishes done yet? Do you realize what time it is?" Mom winced, and the hand that shaded her face turned to massage her forehead.

"I'll get them done." The last time Lena had been inside the kitchen, there wasn't a dirty dish on the counter. How could she have known Mom had spent time in the kitchen?

"This is why you'll never amount to anything." Mom turned to go back inside, pausing at the top of the steps to regain her balance.

Lena clenched the book behind her back. If she were sick like Bessy, Mom would probably run over her instead of doting on her like Nicholas doted on Bessy. What she wouldn't give to have a dad like Nicholas. His addiction to strong drink was too close to home and made her cringe every time she got to those parts, but even with that, deep inside, he at least loved his children.

"Lena!"

Lena shook her thoughts away and followed Mom. As soon as Lena was inside, she wriggled out of the blanket.

North and South slipped from her grasp and landed with a *thud* on the floor, pages bending in weird angles. Lena grabbed it and smoothed out the pages quickly. She may be the only person in Willow Hollow to read this library book, but her carelessness grated on her. Books were meant to be enjoyed for decades.

"Lena Rose!"

The book was torn from her grasp.

"Shoulda guessed." Mom tossed the book in the corner. It landed with a third of the pages curling inward instead of outward.

"Mom!" Lena tried to dart around Mom but was yanked back.

"How did I get such a careless girl? Why couldn't I have gotten a child who—oh, I don't know—helped *pay the bills?*" Mom's grip tightened, and Lena bit back a moan. There would be a bruise there in the morning. Good thing it was winter. Folks at church wouldn't wonder why she wore long sleeves.

"I'm not even sixteen." Lena knew better than to try to free herself from Mom's grip. Once Mom drove her point home, she'd let go. She never hit Lena. Just squeezed and pinched. That was almost worse than a quick slap, though.

"When I was your age…"

Oh yes, when you were my age. Lena's throat tightened, and she lifted her chin. But she couldn't bring herself to meet Mom's searing look.

"When I was your age, I was starting a new life all by myself. Why?" Mom released Lena with a shove.

Lena staggered before she righted herself. She glanced at the book. It would take one of the big dictionaries in the library to get the pages back straight. Maybe two. How was she going to explain this one to Mr. Armstrong? That was the thing—she couldn't.

"Why, girl?"

No one in Willow Hollow really knew how bad things were.

"Answer me!"

But they probably heard the shouting. These walls weren't thick enough to shut out cold air, much less screaming words.

Lena sucked in a sharp breath. *It's the alcohol speaking.* Mom usually wasn't this pushy.

"Lena!"

"It was my fault." There. Mom should be happy and let Lena go do the dishes.

"That's right." Mom flipped her hand and gestured around the room. "Your fault that I live in this—this… *cowshed.*"

Lena turned toward the half of the shack that put forth its best effort to be a kitchen.

"I'm not finished yet, Missy."

Lena spun back around before Mom had the chance to grab her.

"Before you came along, my parents were rich—still are, for all I know. But can I have any of that?" Mom rolled her eyes. "No. You ruined it all."

"I know—"

"I was going to attend college. Do you even know what college is?"

"Of course I—"

"I was accepted into the New York Medical College and Hospital for Women. I could have been a nurse. But instead? I'm here. Nowhere. With no jobs and no opportunities." Mom sank onto the couch—or, the wooden bench she had thrown a few under-stuffed pillows onto to label as such.

"But Mr. Reilly hired—"

"Oh shut up." A curse word slipped from Mom's tongue, searing Lena's ears. She really hoped no neighbors were listening in.

Lena's jaw loosened.

"Stop staring at me. He's a double-crosser. He said the economy was suffering—and he's there sitting pretty. He booted me out."

So that's what this was all about. Mom had lost her job. Again. How long had she kept it this time? A full month?

"If it wasn't for you, child, I could move—be free to go wherever there is a job. I can't hardly afford the bus to get a job in the big city to keep food in your stomach and a coat on your back. And God knows there ain't nothing for me in Willow Hollow worth paying bills."

Lena's eyes slid shut, closing out Mom's angry face. But she couldn't shut out the words. Would never be able to shut out the words. Mom didn't love her—wished she was gone. That way, Mom could live the life she wanted without Lena burdening her.

"Well?" Mom's sharp tone snapped Lena's attention back to her. "Why are you just standing there? That ain't getting anything done. Do the dishes. At least make yourself half useful."

Lena tucked her chin and walked the seven steps to the place they called a kitchen. A washtub sufficed for their sink, firmly planted on a water-stained wooden plank that doubled as a countertop. Just two steps from the washtub was their Acme Princess—it had been one of the cheapest cook stoves at the turn of the century, and whoever had lived in this shed before Mom came along had used it well. Lena was tired of folding aluminum foil to salvage its thin points. One day, the coals were going to decide to fall through the bottom of the sad oven and tumble to the floor. It would probably burn the house down and they'd be forced to move, just like Mom wanted.

Lena poked at the coals inside the stove. Her coat made her clumsy, but she couldn't take it off. Not when there was only a hint of heat coming from inside. She'd just have to wash the dishes in ice water.

The door thudded shut, and Lena spun to look. Through the screen, she could see Mom's bundled-up figure walking away. Lena shut the stove and dashed to retrieve her book. She smoothed its pages the best she could. "I'm sorry. I'll take better care of you." She couldn't have Mr. Armstrong forbidding her to borrow more books—or pay for this one. She'd just sneak in the library first thing Monday morning and spend her day reading in the library while she let these pages be flattened back without Mr. Armstrong's knowledge.

She placed the book under the makeshift couch which doubled as her bed. Mom actually had a room with a bed frame and two-inch mattress. Lena stared after Mom's distant form—walking away from town, not into it. Her gut tightened. Mom was going to visit the Higgins. She didn't need any more of their moonshine. But Mom would do what Mom would do, whether or not it was logical.

With Mom's mind jaded by moonshine, Lena could make an easy getaway. She glanced at the tattered box under the bench. Thanks to the missionary boxes, she had shoes that kept the snow out and an extra dress for Sundays. There wouldn't be much food to bring along. She knew without looking at the open shelves.

She couldn't just run away. Not in dead winter. And not on a Saturday. Everyone tomorrow would be wondering where she went and coming to pester Mom. With a hangover, Mom wouldn't be able to pretend in front of the church folk, and they'd know for sure that they were just poor, lowdown heathens—one of the worst families in Willow Hollow.

Lena shivered and pulled her coat closer as she mentally prepared herself to spend a half hour with her hands half-frozen from icy water. She'd try praying. Pastor Stuart emphasized prayer a lot in his sermons. Something had to change soon, though, or she'd break altogether and make a run for it, logical or not.

2

The screen door bounced lightly shut behind Lena. The calmness that was only in nature surrounded her. Her shoes crushed frozen drops of dew as she left the house behind. Mom was still sleeping. Her sharp words the evening before hadn't kept her awake or from hiding away in her moonshine. But Lena hadn't slept at all. Her mind replayed Mom's words then backtracked to the last time... then the time before that, and all of the times before that. She used to cry herself to sleep, the nights Mom got on her high horse. Not anymore. She was just a few months from sixteen. She had decided it was easier to shut out her feelings against the barrage of words, sheltering her heart from being shredded to pieces.

She should have been prepared for this. Mom had come home more than once this week with her eyes bleary and her speech slightly slurred. But Lena had hidden away from the obvious in the pages of *Ragged Dick*. It wasn't the first book by Alger she had read, but perhaps one of the most exciting.

Her hope rose and ebbed with Dick's as he went from bootblack to respectability. Frugality. That was his secret.

Lena released a sigh and her breath puffed into a white cloud before dissipating. It was impossible to be frugal when Mom spent every extra cent on the devil's drink.

Mom was wayward Lydia from *Pride and Prejudice.* But apparently Mom's family wasn't the Bennet family. And there wasn't any Mr. Darcy to swoop in to rescue them and pay their bills. No Mrs. Bennet to decide to be proud of her unruly daughter instead of shaming her. Who could blame Lena for spending more time with her books than with Mom? At least if the Bennets argued, it was eventually resolved. It didn't dig a huge chasm between them.

"Mornin', Lena. By yourself today?"

Lena looked up. The ground had changed from the dead-brown winter grass to a dust and rock mixture without her realizing she had entered Willow Hollow. "Uh, yes... sir." She slid a smile onto her face and avoided looking Mr. Clark in the eyes. Though, if anyone were to understand the fight between her, Mom, and the moonshine, it would be him. Behind his jolly smile was hidden a long history of hurt. Contentions between the Clarks and the Higgins were nothing new. Rumor had it that the Higgins' moonshine had caused the murder of Mr. Clark's great uncle. Lena wasn't sure how much truth was in the rumor. The mountain folk loved spinning yarns even if they didn't read a lot. Regardless, there were two sides in this town, and unfortunately, Mom sided with the Higgins and their moonshine.

Mr. Clark nodded then continued down Main Street. Not many people were out yet, but give them another ten minutes and they'd make the last rush to service.

Today was Sunday. Church day. Everyone put on their best facade to enter the old, wooden sanctuary and pretend they were all God-fearing folk. Lena had seen Mom do it almost every week that she could remember.

Lena had tried. She had slipped in a few minutes to read a Psalm—the one she went to over and over, in hopes that one day she could fully grasp the words. "I will lift up mine eyes unto the hills..." She knew the passage by heart, but she still read them instead of quoting them. There was something about reading the words—seeing them once again for herself. Straight from God's lips to her heart. "My help cometh from the Lord which made heaven and earth."

That was the beauty of words. She had hidden away in the world of letters and symbols when Mr. Armstrong had unlocked the door to their meaning, after Aunt Melba Lynn's death, God rest her soul. *The Little Princess, Robinson Crusoe, Jane Eyre, Pride and Prejudice...* while they had been hearty companions, they really didn't compare to God's Holy Word. Sure, there were truths explored in works of fiction. But in the Bible... in the Bible, they weren't just words on a page. It was a promise, to her, for today. She would cling to that promise until she could fully believe it.

Mom didn't understand that beauty, though. She scoffed at Lena for reading God's Word and accused her of trying to be ultra-spiritual when she caught Lena with the Bible.

Lena shook free from the depressing thoughts and slipped into the church building. Pastor Stuart was in the front, talking with Mrs. Cora Lee, their organist. Lena found the third to last wooden bench and quietly sat against the wall. She closed her eyes, letting herself fly away with the carefree birds that twittered outside the windows as they went about their tasks. What would it be like to pass through trees and up the Appalachians in freedom?

With a sigh, she opened her eyes as footsteps came toward her. She forced another smile, this time for Pastor Stuart. It was a little easier, looking into his round face and blue eyes. He was tall, but he never seemed imposing. He was too friendly for that.

"How is your mom today, Lena?"

"She's feeling poorly. A headache." Lena had practice shading the truth after all these years.

Genuine concern creased in Pastor Stuart's face. "I'm sorry to hear that." It was likely Pastor Stuart assumed the meaning behind her words, but he didn't ask and she didn't explain further. "How has her job been holding out for her?"

She knew the depths behind that question. Every week, it felt as if they were all holding their breath to see who would be sacked next. It had been the economic plague since before Lena had entered her double digits, and there wasn't hope of it relinquishing yet. She glanced around the small building. Just a couple of people were here, chatting softly. They would all know soon enough. Everyone in Willow Hollow tended to know everyone's business quickly. Still, she lowered her voice. "She was… let go." Fired. Again.

When would she get used to saying these words? It was at least the twelfth time in the past two years, but they still stung sharply.

There was no condemnation in Pastor Stuart's blue eyes and his brows furrowed beneath his curly brown hair. "I'm sorry, Lena."

What else could he have said? It served Mom right for being such a flapper? Lena cringed as the word crossed her mind. It wasn't the type of language the pastor would use. Even if it was true.

"Hey, Curt!"

Lena felt guilt rush through her, even though Mr. Armstrong had no clue about the condition of *North and South*. He wouldn't know, either, if she could help it.

"What were you telling me yesterday about the president's idea?"

"Oh, yes sir." Mr. Armstrong nodded to the pastor. "WPA, that is, Works Progress Administration, is an idea to open up more employment to folks. All the details were finalized last week for our library to be a part. Tomorrow we'll put the paper out for hiring."

Pastor Stuart turned to Lena with a smile. "Isn't that God's providence? Here is a job, ready and waiting."

Lena tried to smile back, but her face felt frozen. Mom? In the library? She was glad the rush of church folk entered the doors just then, hiding her emotions in a swirl of conversation and greetings that took Pastor Stuart away from her.

No. The library was Lena's one safe haven—her only true home. It was just one of the rooms in the Building, yes, but still. Every day that Mr. Armstrong had the library open, Lena was there, finding a new book, revisiting old ones, escaping from the pain of reality as long as she could.

Lena scooted even closer to the wall as a family filed onto the bench beside her. She caught Mr. Armstrong's glance from across the room and he gave her a friendly grin. If Mom worked at the library, Lena couldn't spend hours in there, soaking in the words. She wouldn't feel comfortable chatting with the librarian about what she had read.

I can do it.

The thought jolted Lena and her pulse quickened. What if this was her answer? She replayed the conversation between Pastor and Mr. Armstrong in her mind as she stood to join the congregation in a hymn. A job in the library would be almost a dream come true. She'd have a way to make money and prove to Mom that she wasn't useless. She could begin saving money for being out on her own as soon as possible.

"Please be seated."

Lena jerked her attention to Pastor Stuart and followed the congregation. Maybe Pastor was right. Maybe it was God's providence—just not for Mom. Lena couldn't focus as Pastor Stuart began preaching. Her mind raced ahead. She'd be sure she was the first one in the Building tomorrow.

3

*M*om was still sleeping. Lena slid *North and South* under her coat. As cold as it was inside, she probably needed the extra layer of her blanket for her walk through town. But that would look tacky. She already looked bad enough in her tattered coat and frayed skirt. She could be worse off, though. She had woolen knee socks, and that helped. It didn't matter that the heel was out in one of them. Her shoe covered that, and no one was the wiser.

She looked at her shadow on the screen door. Her brown hair was down, as always. It reached well below her shoulders—not at all like Mom's hair. When she was sober, Mom spent hours on her hair—creating model-worthy finger waves and loose curls. She had her hair down to perfection, with pristine waves accentuating her face. But Lena's hair? Mom was constantly pointing out how it was drab and styleless the way Lena let it hang loose and natural. That, when Mom was Lena's age, she had taken care to present herself as an embodiment of the modern woman—and, given Mom's beaus, she had succeeded well.

Lena smoothed the top where annoying frizzes danced freely. There was hair product she could use to help that, of course. She straightened her shoulders and swung open the door, leaving her reflection behind. Hair product cost money—and when she had her own money, she wasn't going to spend it on such frivolity.

She clutched *North and South,* safely hidden from sight, as she traipsed around the shacks clustered near her home. Everything was frozen this morning. A few wisps of smoke attempted their mockery against the cold, but Lena knew everyone inside those buildings was just as cold as she was outside. Hopefully the library would be open by now. Still, it was always warmer in the Building than in Lena's shack, so waiting there wouldn't be terrible.

Mr. Armstrong was putting the key in the library door when she walked in the main door of the Building.

"Hello, Lena. You're up early."

Lena nodded her reply and stood a few feet away from Mr. Armstrong, waiting for him to get the door open.

"You're ready for another book already—I mean, you've already finished? Didn't I just give you one?"

Lena pressed a smile onto her lips and tightened her grip on *North and South.* How did she think she was going to get it under some heavy books without Mr. Armstrong's notice? She'd have to distract him—thoroughly. "I did finish it." She stepped inside after him and squinted in the darkness of the room.

"You'll have to wait while I get things going." Mr. Armstrong put a few logs in the small stove before walking

26

through the small room that held a world of knowledge and adventure. "I expect the library to be busy today, what with a new job opening."

A new job? Only one? Lena took a deep breath and blurted out, "I'd like to apply."

Mr. Armstrong spun around, his easy smile slipping from his face as his brown eyes studied her. "Lena, I know you like books… that is, you have the passion for the job."

Lena's gut tightened. There was a "but" coming. She knew it. She shouldn't have even tried. Should've known better than to assume she'd get the first job she ever wanted. She turned to go—somewhere. It was humiliating to stay here under Mr. Armstrong's scrutiny.

"That is, I thought your mom would want to apply."

Lena swallowed. "Mom hates books." She could only assume Mom's passion against them had something to do with her spoiled dream of college.

"Well then…" The way Mr. Armstrong's voice raised in pitch gave her the smallest glimmer of hope. She turned back to him, but kept her gaze from his.

"Lena, I guess you can be the first to fill out an application."

Application. Of course. Still, it was something. Instead of hope surging forward, a plethora of other emotions drowned her. What would Mom say when she found out Lena had applied for a job? Or when she realized that Lena didn't tell her of a local opening?

"Give me just a few minutes…" Mr. Armstrong busied himself at the desk, and Lena slipped to the short bookshelf at the opposite corner.

No one used dictionaries much around here. She slid *North and South* between the two old volumes, satisfied that the pressure would help the pages settle back to normal.

"Are you coming?"

Lena slipped away from the books, hoping a day would be enough time to straighten the pages and return the book to its rightful place. Mr. Armstrong wouldn't be looking here for it. She had spent countless hours in here. She knew his habits.

"Do you know how to ride a horse or mule?"

The first question from her first potential employer. She had experienced the emotions and turmoil of so many different aspects of life here in the library. But her first possible job? She had to focus. "Yes." Last summer, little Mary Stuart, the pastor's youngest daughter, had convinced her older brother Jed to take the horse out. While Mary pretended to give Lena riding lessons, it was thirteen-year-old Jed who had really been of help. If there was a library where she could borrow horses for free, Lena wouldn't know how to split her time between books and horses. But... "Why do I need to?"

"Oh." Mr. Armstrong tugged at his faded tweed suit. He turned to his desk and pulled out a paper. "The job available is for travel."

Lena caught herself before giving way to surprise. She had to act confident and sure of herself or Mr. Armstrong wouldn't take her seriously.

"Sit. That is, this will take a moment to explain." He gave Lena one of his smiles as she sat on the edge of the chair in front of the desk. "I'm still working on the routes, but plans are to hire three ladies…" He paused at that word and glanced at Lena. She squirmed. She was old enough, wasn't she? "…to bring the library to those in the mountains who cannot come. We want them to be from Willow Hollow—folks that the mountain folk can trust. You know how they are with strangers."

Lena kept herself from squirming. Sure, she had seen a highlander here or there in town, but she wasn't ever really out and about. She couldn't list the names of those who lived in the mountains or just on the other side of town. Mr. Armstrong probably didn't know that.

"We're getting our first donation shipment of books specifically to expand our library for this program," Mr. Armstrong glanced up at the clock that hung above the desk, "in about two hours. In fact, even if you don't get the job, we could use your help unloading the books. I can't offer pay—"

"I'll do it." Anything to prove she was hardy and strong enough for whatever this job was that Mr. Armstrong had in mind.

He grinned at her. "Well thank you, Dear." He cleared his throat and pushed the paper closer to her. "You can fill this out, and I'll look through all applications this week."

He didn't say it in so many words, but Lena knew—her chances at getting this job were slim.

"Do you have any questions?"

Lena looked down at the paper she had automatically grabbed. "When will I know if I have the job?"

Mr. Armstrong gave her a smile. "You really want it, don't you?"

"More than anything!" The words rushed from Lena. The library wasn't much of a place for talking, but if it got her the job and a position away from Mom, she'd do all the talking she could. "We need the money—Mom lost her job. I can do this. I love books. I—I love horses." What else could she say? Mr. Armstrong's smile didn't waver. That was hopeful at least. "I—I am a fast learner." At least, she thought she was. She had learned many things by herself. What else did Mr. Armstrong say the job entailed? Bringing the library to the mountains? "I'm not scared of the mountains." Or, she guessed she wasn't. She hadn't been there much. "I'm sure I can—"

Mr. Armstrong held up a hand. "My dear, fill out the application."

Lena swallowed back tears and looked down at the paper. She mechanically grabbed a pen from Mr. Armstrong's desk and stilled her trembling hand so she could fill in her name.

"Lena."

She cleared her face from emotion and looked up at Mr. Armstrong.

He gave her a friendly wink. "Let's see how you do at unloading books later today."

4

$\mathcal{I}$t was still dark when Lena left her home. The first Monday in February—the first day on the trail. The first day of the Library program. The first official day of her new job. Butterflies lifted Lena's spirits and she skipped a few times before remembering she was outside. If there were any early risers, they'd see her. She was a responsible adult now—she had a job, and she intended to keep it. But she couldn't be late. She didn't quite run, but it definitely wasn't a walk as she wove her way through the cluster of houses to Main Street. Mr. Armstrong had stressed starting early so she'd have enough daylight to go through the entire route.

Guilt rippled through her. She still hadn't told Mom. Then again, with the busyness of the library this last week, helping Mr. Armstrong with the books for the mountain folk, gleaning the information she needed to know on the trail, and getting more practice in riding, she had barely been home. And Mom hadn't asked why. Lena would have told her. Maybe. For a brief moment, she wished Aunt Melba Lynn was still alive. She would have at least listened to

Lena's excitement, even if she wouldn't have given much input. As it was, Lena had tried to keep it from bubbling over as she spent hours at the library shadowing Mr. Armstrong. He was swell, letting her hound him with questions. And he had accepted her for the position! Well, it wasn't a positive position, he had said. He had taken on a brotherly look as he had said he wanted to be sure she could handle three routes in one week. She could. She knew she could. Mr. Armstrong had said there were two other ladies taking routes, and she was willing to prove herself as capable as either of them.

Lena gave another skip as she entered Main Street. That was enough childish antics, though. She took in a deep breath, letting the cold air sting her lungs. It was slightly warmer today—temperatures would rise above freezing as the sun warmed the mountains. Still cold, but bearable. Especially with anticipation warming her through.

She forced herself to walk up the porch steps to the Building one at a time. She just wanted to skip two at a time—had wanted to all last week, but there was no telling whose eyes were on her in town.

This was it. She placed her hand on the doorknob and turned. It stuck in position. She tried again. Surely she wasn't here before Mrs. Branson opened up the Building. She looked up at the skyline. It had to be near five o'clock, and that was when Mr. Armstrong said to be here. But then, she didn't have a watch to tell the time. Maybe with her first paycheck she could buy one from Sears & Roebuck. She still couldn't wrap her mind around it. Twenty-eight dollars a month! That was a full ten dollars more than Mom had made last month.

It was a fortune during this crisis the nation faced. And it would be hers to decide how to spend. Lena bit back her smile as she started pacing the porch. Now the cold was getting to her. She rubbed her hands together. One dollar and sixty cents a month to rent a horse from Pastor Stuart's livery. Then she really ought to buy some yarn for gloves. She'd read enough stories of people who had lost fingers due to frostbite. She'd just have to keep them close to the horse's warmth until she got some. But a watch? That would be frivolity, not necessity. At least, not yet.

Where are you, Mr. Armstrong? She walked off the porch and back onto Main Street. It had been a good ten minutes by now, she was sure. She crossed the street to the livery, angled across from the Building. Jed had shown her how to brush and saddle Kirby. Pastor Stuart said she could get him any time she needed him. She entered the open livery and felt around. She hadn't quite expected it to be this dark when she practiced saddling Kirby last week. But she had done it every day. She could figure it out.

She brought the saddle to Kirby's stall.

"Good morning, boy." Her voice sounded loud joining the horses' quiet movements. "Ready for a full day?" She ran her fingers over his forehead, just barely making out the star under his forelock. She opened the door and led him out. As she saddled him up, she kept glancing over her shoulder. The sky was melting from deep blue into bold hues of purple and gold. It was going to be a clear day today. She smiled. A hint of God's blessings on her first day on the job.

She checked the cinch and made sure Kirby hadn't done his dirty trick of holding his breath while she tightened it. Everything looked good.

"Are you ready?" Lena was. More than ready. She grabbed the reins and clucked for Kirby to follow her. He was gentle and amiable. The perfect horse for this task. Both Pastor Stuart and Jed agreed that he would do well for Lena. Which was good, because she wasn't as confident about her horsewoman skills as she pretended to be. Riding on Main Street was one thing. Keeping her balance while Kirby picked his way up the mountain slope would be something completely different.

"Morning!"

Finally. Lena gave Mr. Armstrong a smile.

"Perfect timing. Come on and get your pack. Did you pack some food? You'll be hungry, come lunchtime."

Lena gave a slight nod. But it wasn't lunch she had packed. It was breakfast, because she hadn't eaten yet. Her stomach was too excited—and the longer she held off breakfast, the better she would last until she was home again to eat supper.

"You remember your route?"

"Yes… sir." She often forgot that Mr. Armstrong was almost twice her age. He was no longer just the librarian who chatted with her about books and stories they both loved. He was her boss, and she needed to respect his position in addition to his age.

Lena followed him through the Building to the library. On Saturday, they had packed the satchels she was to bring today. Sunday School pamphlets for the children, *Women's Home Companion* for women, old copies of *Life* magazine for adults, plus a collection of novels—*Rebecca of Sunnybrook Farm, Oliver Twist, Macbeth,* and *David*

Copperfield were just a few of those she had slipped in. Their selection had grown with the seventy-eight books that were brought to them from the city, and Mr. Armstrong was beyond excited for a start to their Packhorse Librarian program, claiming it was only the beginning of donations and sharing.

Mr. Armstrong handed the packed saddlebags over to her. "You remember today's route?"

It was the second time he had asked, but Lena ignored it. "Northeast toward Cedar Valley. Start on the trail, cross Franklin Creek. There's a good dozen shacks to start with." She had rehearsed the directions in her mind ever since Mr. Armstrong had decided her Monday route. Wednesday and Friday, she had two different routes.

"Remember, the trail becomes a little rocky path. But you can see where it cuts clearly."

Lena shifted the pack, keeping most of its weight on the desk she stood beside. Good thing Kirby was the one lugging these uphill. She wouldn't be able to make it out of Willow Hollow with such a load.

"Head back by four o'clock so you're here again before dark. The folks are friendly, but the animals—that is…" Mr. Armstrong flashed her a smile, as if that would cause her to forget the fact of wildlife. She knew about the animals in the mountain ranges. Usually, if one let well enough alone, the animals would return to their business in peace. "We just want to be sure you're safe." He winked at her. "It will spare me your mom's worry." He chuckled as he glanced out the window.

Lena forced a smile. What if Mom found out about her job from someone else? She swallowed and followed Mr. Armstrong's gaze. The surrounding areas were still a milky gray in the morning's shadows, but not for long.

"I'd better get going." She patted the books and this time offered a real smile.

"Wait." Mr. Armstrong rushed to his desk and opened the drawer. He pulled out something red. "Don't want to freeze those fingers or you'd just be one day on the job." He brought a pair of mittens over to her and thrust them in her hands. "That is, stay warm. Be safe."

Lena's throat tightened as her fingers wrapped around the coarse wool of men's mittens. "Uh… thank… you." It was the proper thing to say, but it felt like so little compared to the gift he had just bestowed on her.

"And I'll have you a set of keys to the Building by Wednesday, so you can start on the trail earlier—and have access for the days I'm in the city's library."

She took a few steps toward the door. She couldn't take any more of Mr. Armstrong's thoughtfulness today or she'd burst into tears. "Thank you. I'll—I'll be sure to leave these on your desk tonight." She held up the mittens.

Mr. Armstrong shook his head. "They're yours now. That is… it's a part of your uniform. An employee perk." He winked and waved her off.

"Thank you." Lena nodded and turned to leave. The sacks were heavy, but inside, her heart floated—she barely remembered walking the length through the Building to Kirby.

"Here we are," Lena whispered. She attached the saddle bags to the saddle like Jed had shown her. It was possible the books would get banged around, but considering these were already beaten-up leftovers from bigger cities, Lena wouldn't have to worry much about that. The material was still good, even if some of the covers were torn or ripped off altogether. She double-checked to make sure the saddle was secure, then mounted. She slipped the mittens onto her hands and wriggled her fingers inside the shield against the cold before taking the reins. A slight flick of her wrist, and Kirby's head turned away from the Building. His steps were steady and sure as he walked down Main Street then onto a side path.

It felt good—to be up and about before the bus roared its way across the river to pick up commuters. The town was still asleep, and she was setting off on her first grand adventure. She placed her hands serenely on the saddle horn. Before long, she'd have to cling to it as Kirby picked his way up steep inclines. But for now, everything was calm and relaxed.

She glanced around, and her eyes caught a glimpse of a curtain dropping down. Prickles and tension instantly attacked the serenity Lena was feeling. Widow Ida Burman. Even without having met the woman's serious, no-nonsense brown eyes, she could just sense the thoughts that must be running under the wisps of grayish-white hair. Widow Burman had an opinion about everyone and everything—and her seeing a woman leaving town on horseback this early in the day... Lena shuddered as she could almost hear the woman's accusations. *You're going to be just like your mom. Who are your friends? If you spent more time with those who lived uprightly...*

No one in Willow Hollow had ever verbalized their thoughts, but Lena had felt them in all the silent stares she had received since childhood. Willow Hollow was a tight-knit community, but Mom had invaded the community sixteen years ago when her parents had sent her here, and even though Lena had been here all her life, she still wasn't part of the clan. Always the outsider. Always the one whose every action would be scoured, scrubbed clean, and left to dry. Not everyone thought that way—the pastor's family was kind to her, and Mr. Armstrong, of course. Everyone was polite as mountain folk politeness went. But Lena still wasn't one of *them*—born and raised with a father and mother, nurtured by loving grandparents…

Lena shifted in the saddle as Kirby's feet crunched the loose rocks. If she couldn't create a good life inside Willow Hollow, and especially in the four flimsy walls of her own home, she certainly would do her best to create one as a book lady on the Cumberland Plateau. She wasn't going to let the ugly glare of one woman—or half the community, for that matter—violate the dreams and hopes she clung to today.

5

*T*he sun was well overhead when Kirby shifted from climbing uphill to straighter terrain. Lena sighed as she let her body straighten and relax. If it wasn't for Kirby's agility, she would rather walk these mountainous trails than trust a horse's four feet. Jed had assured her she'd learn to trust Kirby more the more time she spent with him. She hoped so. The first building appeared—if it could be called such. It was some construction of wood and sheet metal with tarp flapping in the chilling breeze. Lena pulled back on the reins. A little child—maybe four years old—darted behind the tarp, and Lena could hear murmurs.

Her heart sped up. Should she dismount? Stay on top of Kirby? What if they came out with scowls? Mr. Armstrong had warned her that not everyone had appreciated President Roosevelt's efforts to educate the illiterate. Maybe they would be like Mom and scorn the books she so dearly loved.

She had thought over the scenarios hundreds of times in the hours she rode up here, and still, she didn't have a plan of action. She didn't want to be Margaret Hale and assume the poor wanted help. In fact, it was good she had just finished reading *North and South*. From everything she had heard whispered in Willow Hollow, these mountain people were much like the proud folks Margaret had faced in Milton—they might look needy, but they were self-sufficient in their own way. She wouldn't presume they needed her help. She would just show them how wonderful books were. Surely that wouldn't offend.

A woman shorter than Lena lifted the tarp and shouted out, "Whatya needin'? Surely ya ain't lost this high up."

"No… ma'am…" Lena decided to slide down from the horse. It seemed strange to address an uncouth, boisterous woman with propriety, but she would do the best she could. "I'm from Willow Hollow."

Too mechanic. Too impersonal. Lena took in a shuddering breath then said nothing. She didn't know what to say—or what was expected of her to say.

The woman still hadn't come out of her shack. "And what're ye doin' here?"

"I…" Any planning or preparations of speech-making fled from Lena's mind. She glanced down at her red mittened hands.

"I ain't got time for jabbin'."

"Yes ma'am." Lena slipped her mittens off and opened the sack nearest her. She bent a page as she jerked something from the sack. "I'm a book lady. That is, I have books for your children." Great. Now she was sounding like Mr. Armstrong.

"We don't need books." The flap was pulled down, hiding the woman.

Lena wasn't going to push the matter. Didn't know how. She swallowed and looked at Kirby. He was staring straight ahead, not concerned with her business. She took the reins and led him beyond the first shack. Another stood about four yards away—or leaned, more like it. Lena would count her place a blessing after today. Mom had always said their shed was nothing, but they at least had four solid walls. And a door.

She hesitated when no one came out then cleared her throat. No one acknowledged her. "Excuse me? Hello?"

Still nothing.

Should she write a note?

Her stomach convulsed and she steadied herself against Kirby. Visions of a dozen children happily flocking to her, sitting at her feet while she read them the *Tales of Peter Rabbit*, loving the colorful and quaint illustrations as she did, were buried in stony silence. She bit her lower lip. Elinor in *Sense and Sensibility* had never given up this easily when faced with difficulty. She wouldn't either.

She couldn't quite see the next shack, but she had done enough riding for now. Wise as it was that Pastor Stuart suggested she spend a few hours on Kirby last week, practicing near Willow Hollow was nothing like this journey up the mountainside.

The path narrowed in front of her and sliced between two boulders. "Can you make it, Kirb?" Lena whispered, trying to put some positivity in her voice. She led the way, and Kirby followed her, fully trusting.

She heard the children before she saw them—shouting, laughing, some crying. They weren't timid like the first one she had met—rather, these would seem kin to the woman who shouted out her questions. Lena pasted on a smile. She'd had enough practice smiling when it felt like the last thing she wanted to do. Hopefully today it would read convincingly.

"Good morning!" Her voice sounded unnaturally cheery, even to herself. She smiled even bigger as six children froze and all noise hushed. She noticed sticks strewn across the way, making shapes almost like rooms. "Are you playing make-believe?"

The biggest of the group stood to her feet. "Yeah. Did ye lost yourself?"

Lena didn't have to force the grin that came. "No, I'm here on purpose." An idea threaded through her mind. "I like make-believe too. Did you know there are whole *books* written on make-believe?" This was exciting—a natural connection to the children.

The eldest stuck out her chin and folded her arms in front of her. "What'd I care?"

"Oh, but they're marvelous things!" Lena looked down at the book she had never put back in the sack. A *Popular Mechanics* magazine. That wouldn't interest them. She shoved it in the sack and pulled out an actual book. *Pollyanna*. That was more like it. "Ah, here is a book about a little girl—probably about your age—and she liked to play a happy game."

One of the boys widened his blue eyes as he stared at the book. "What's that?"

"This?" Lena held it out for them to see. The whole group jerked backwards. "This is *Pollyanna.*"

"No, *this* be Pollyanna." The boy stuck his thumb toward the tiniest girl. She looked no more than two years old, but she nodded wisely as if she knew more than her size accounted for.

Lena bit back a laugh. "Do you want to hear about another girl named—"

"Who're you?"

Lena jerked as she realized someone else had joined them. The question came from a man Mom would call the "rugged good-lookin' type." Lena gritted her teeth at her wayward thought and backed toward Kirby as if he could protect her. "I—I came to bring books."

"Don't got money for food. Why'd we trash it on books?"

"Oh! No… sir. Not for sale. They're from the library. The library loans the books. You select a book or two and next week—"

"I ain't never heard the likes. Ain't none of us want books nohow."

Lena felt like one of the children, bowing to his commandeering voice. She lowered her eyes to the ground. "I'll go on my way then." She kept by Kirby's side while she nudged him forward, placing him between her and the man.

"Smith's ain't gonna want 'em neither. Don't even try."

It was polite to say "thank you" or "yes, sir," but Lena knew if she opened her mouth, tears would start to fall. She'd pass by the Smith's then and go to the next hut. Surely "third time's the charm" would work here? If not… would Mr. Armstrong really make her do it again next week? This was to be her Monday route.

She avoided the next shack and kept going. The next shack she came upon—no, there were three shacks. Almost stacked on top of each other. She couldn't just pass them up, as much as she wanted to. Three women knelt in front of three washtubs, their hands red as they rubbed clothes up and down ribbed sheets of metal. A baby squalled from one of the shacks, but Lena couldn't guess which mother it belonged to—they were all indifferent.

She reached inside a sack and dug out a *Women's Home Companion.* Here was a group of homemakers. Perhaps they could be interested in the pictures and articles.

"Hello." Unlike the cheery greeting Lena had offered just minutes before, this one came out apologetic. "I'm here for the library—with the library." She blurted out the words that had raised questions in the man just before. "We're giving free books and magazines for your pleasure." That was tacky.

The women looked up, their hands not slowing. They had to be sisters. Their hair was the same dusty brown, their eyes the same molasses color. And their faces held the same distrustful straight lines.

"This is a magazine that shows helpful ways to do things around the house."

The lady with the most wrinkles gave a harsh laugh. "Girl, we ain't got enough of a *house* to do with. That ain't gonna help us none."

"Well, we also have…" Lena turned to look in her sack. But not before she caught the interest spark in the middle woman's eyes.

"No."

Lena jumped at the harsh word uttered by the eldest woman. "N-no?"

The woman nodded. "Don't know why city folk think they can come sell wares."

"But it's not for sale. It's free. For loan."

"An' we don't take no charity. I done said no. Now git afore you annoy all the likes of me."

As if the woman wasn't already annoyed. Lena didn't want to stay and find out. She tucked the magazine back in the sack. The sack that had just as many books as when she set out this morning. What would she say to Mr. Armstrong? That her first day was a failure? She couldn't help but feel this week was a test-run anyway. He had hired her, but she knew he had more than an ounce of hesitancy hidden behind his congenial smile.

It took everything in her to smile and wave goodbye. Hoping she wouldn't have to see them again. Suddenly realizing that she would—this evening when she retraced her trail back home. Her shoulders slumped and she counted her steps walking beside Kirby. She'd get through the day somehow.

"Miss? Miss!"

Lena turned slightly toward the voice—enough to see if the call was directed to her or someone else.

"Book lady!"

That could mean no one else. Lena's hand tightened on the reins. "Sir?"

There was a building—actually built from planks of wood with a secure door—hidden behind the trio she had just passed by. An elderly man stood in front of it, waving a faded gray knit hat. "You said you have books? To lend?"

He took a few steps toward her. "I'll take some of your books, miss."

Lena leaned against Kirby and burst into tears.

6

 *T*he name's Homer Reed." The elderly man had waited until Lena dried her tears before speaking. Now, he was beside her, courteously looking at the saddle packs, not at her tear-filled eyes.

"I-I'm sorry, sir." Lena sucked in a shaky breath and pressed her mittens to her eyes. "Mr. Reed." She rounded Kirby and opened the sack on the other side. These books would be more like those a man would appreciate. She had to act somewhat professional—to redeem her first impression. "What do you like reading? Carpentry? Fiction?" She swallowed as the questions left her mouth. Mr. Armstrong had mentioned that some of the folks perhaps didn't know how to read. If so, then she'd just insulted this man and he might change his mind.

"Lemme see what ya have. If'n you have time."

"Yes, sir." She was already ahead of schedule, now that the first few families had rejected her offerings. But she could see the younger of the washerwomen sneaking a glance her way. Maybe in time others would warm up to the idea after all. She untied the whole sack from the saddle.

"Here, lemme take that. Come inside. It at least knocks off the wind. And you can meet my bride, Nora."

He didn't give her much choice but strode toward the cottage and held the door open for her.

"Nora, we got us some company!"

"Company?" A quivery voice asked the question. "Who is it?"

Mr. Reed looked at Lena as she passed into the dark interior. "Forgive me, miss, I didn't ask after your name."

Lena gave a half-smile in forgiveness and offered, "Lena. Or just the book lady." She liked the ring to that—something new that separated her from the name Mom had bestowed upon her at birth.

"What's a book lady?" The soft voice belonged to a slender woman in the corner, whom Lena assumed was Nora Reed, nestled in a once-overstuffed chair that was now limp from decades of use.

"She's got books from a library."

"Oh, yes. Come in." Mrs. Reed grasped the head of the cane beside her and pulled herself to her feet. She hobbled toward the stove in the corner that looked as decrepit as Lena's own Acme Princess. "We have tea." She opened a tin and took out a limp bag that had probably been used a dozen times before. "I keep forgetting how long to let it set." She set a kettle on the stove and gave a little laugh. "My memory ain't what it was."

"Just set it 'til the water's brown, Honey." Mr. Reed gave his wife a patient smile. He motioned to a hardback wooden chair. "Please take a seat, our little book lady, and let's see what ya have." He set the sack cautiously on the table. "Can I get the other sack?"

"Well, I suppose…" She glanced toward Mrs. Reed. "Yes, there will be books that may interest your wife."

"Wonderful." Mr. Reed left the door open as he sauntered outside.

Lena opened the sack and began pulling out the books. She placed the magazines in one stack and books in another. She felt Mrs. Reed behind her and turned to give a timid smile.

"What are those?"

Lena straightened the stack of books. "We have fictional books, educational books, and magazines." Her hand slowed on the cover of *Pilgrim's Progress*. It was one of the first books she had read, and still held a special place in her heart.

Mr. Reed came in and secured the door. With an actual glass window, it wasn't too dark in the room.

"Now, lemme see your wares."

Lena steadied her hands before she knocked over a stack of books. He was really interested. She was going to return to Mr. Armstrong with at least one positive report.

"Well, we have some of *The American Thresherman*." She laid the two tattered magazines in front of him then offered, "Mrs. Reed may be interested in *The Farmer's Wife* magazine." Lena used to spend hours flipping through the suggestions of how to add color to homes and daydreaming of the vastness that was promised in Oregon.

"Well, well…" Mr. Reed chuckled. "But please, miss, call us just Homer and Nora. Don't need to get all fancy on us. Right, Nora?"

Mrs. Reed—or Nora—nodded in agreement. Homer held his arm out to her. "Let's get you settled back down. I'll see to the tea."

"The tea?" Nora glanced back at the stove.

"Yes, Honey. I'll make the tea." He helped lower Nora into her chair then tucked a blanket firmly around her. "Now, miss, what reading books ya got? I don't mind the magazines, but what I really like is a good story to keep me on edge these cold winter days—ya know?"

Lena couldn't stop the smile—it seemed to bubble up from her heart and erupted short of a giggle. "What kind of story do you like?"

"Surprise me."

She looked down at the stacks of books and magazines. She didn't know this man. How was she to know what he would like? He was probably fifty years her senior—what did men even like to read? She picked up the two Jane Austen's. They were all about women and luxury and marriage. She chewed her lower lip. *Pollyanna* was for children. A hardcover book nestled underneath it. She pulled it out—the tan cover with black and red imprints woven around it brought a smile to her face.

"What's this one?" Homer asked.

"*The Merry Adventures of Robin Hood.* Have you read it?"

"Honey, I haven't read anything in decades. Even if I'd read it as a boy, I'd read it again."

Lena held the book out to him. With the edges of the covers only slightly frayed, it was one of the best editions they had in the library sacks.

"What d'ya like about it?" Homer patted the book gently before laying is on the opposite end of the table. "Lemme check the tea while ya tell me."

Lena glanced over at the book. "Howard Pyle is funny." She hesitated before venturing, "I... I had to hide a laugh many times." She didn't even tell these details to Mr. Armstrong, but she desperately wanted Homer to enjoy the book.

Homer brought a Mason jar with amber liquid to Lena. "I like humor. Nora does too, don't ya, Honey?" He turned to bring a second jar of tea to his wife.

"Oh, yes." Nora gave her husband a smile as she took the tea.

Lena noticed that Homer sat back down at the table without any tea himself. She glanced back at the stove, but there was no more tea to be had. She took a sip. The liquid was warm, but not hot. "Thank you." She smiled at Homer, hoping to convey that she realized the sacrifice his hospitality was. "It has been years since I've had tea." Since Aunt Melba Lynn was living, to be exact. And her tea was strong and sweet—not watery and plain. But Aunt Melba was gone before the stock market crashed.

"You're welcome. Now, about this library plan of yourn... how far do ya plan on goin' today?"

Lena shrugged, not quite sure if it was time to repack the sacks or just sit and chat. "I'll be heading back down the mountain before dark."

"Would ya like some company?" Homer's light blue eyes twinkled, though his lips didn't turn up in a smile. "Mountain folk don't take too kindly to strangers—even if'n they see ya in church or at the store once in a while. An' some of 'em still can't speak English none too well. They're still keepin' close to their mother country of Scotland."

Lena swallowed. Mr. Armstrong had mentioned that her routes would be easier because these folks came to town— she had just let him assume that she'd be a familiar face to them. She didn't realize the repercussions it would have. She was glad she was already sitting down—her legs didn't feel like they would support her right now. A mixture of tears and happiness overflowed her. "Yes, sir. Please." Surely with such a friendly granddad accompanying her, she would receive a much warmer welcome than before.

"Well…" Homer patted *Robin Hood* and stood to his feet. "Lemme get Ruthie to check in on Nora." He raised his voice slightly. "Nora, I'll be goin' out fer a bit. You're fine here?"

Nora looked up, her gaze slowly focusing from the blank stare she'd had. "I'm fine."

"Now, while you pack up those books, lemme get Nora settled." And Homer was out the door.

Lena bit back a smile as she slipped the magazines into the rough sack. Then the children's books. Then the others. Hope began to spark in her heart—just a small glow, but surely with the mountain-folk's interest, it would fan that flame. She could prove to Mr. Armstrong that she was worthy to keep this job bestowed on her.

7

$\mathcal{L}$ena's head sank lower with each mile Kirby picked his way downhill. Monday she had returned with a glowing report to give to Mr. Armstrong. A whole dozen books were lent out after Homer had gone with her. Wednesday and today however… only one curious child had allowed her to read *Peter Rabbit* to him on Wednesday, then begged his mom to let him keep it until next week. Today, she couldn't even boast that much success. She had only seen glimpses of a few children. They didn't speak to her when she greeted them. Instead, they had turned and run. The adults were no better. No one today was willing to give her even a minute of their time to listen to what she had to offer.

The misty rain cloaked her with a drab gray feeling, like Margaret Hale had with the drabness of northern territory. Loneliness. Failure. Confusion. Lena wished she hadn't returned *North and South* to the library—almost as smooth and compact as when she had first borrowed it. She could probably get it back out, but she wanted it now—tonight. And she wouldn't be in Willow Hollow until after Mr.

Armstrong had left. She knew how to fill out borrows, but it went against protocol for her to do it herself. She'd just wait.

Willow Hollow was silent when she entered it—just like it had been the other nights of her routes—except tonight it was accompanied by that droning drizzle. Lena stopped in front of the Building and dismounted. She slipped a key from her pocket. It had given her a sense of responsibility, that day when Mr. Armstrong handed it to her. Now, she felt like she was failing that responsibility. For one person—like Mom—to reject books she could understand. But for dozens of people to do so? When they were freely handed to them? It must be her. She stuck the key in the keyhole and turned it until that satisfactory *click* indicated the job was done. She knew the way through the Building to the library well in this darkness. Once in the library, she set the sacks by Mr. Armstrong's desk. Just as full as when she had packed them yesterday.

She retraced her steps back to Kirby and led him across the street to the stables. A lantern glowed inside.

"Evening, Lena."

She wasn't expecting anyone. She froze as the greeting registered in her mind. Jed.

Lena nodded at him. "Evening." She started toward Kirby's stall but Jed grabbed the reins from her.

"I can do it."

She would readily welcome the help—Tuesday and Thursday hadn't given her enough real rest in between each long day of riding and rejection. But she had bartered with Pastor Stuart's price, and instead of spending fifty cents a week, she only had to pay forty, if she was willing to help care for the horse. She wasn't going to let Jed pull some of her load. Lena felt her face flush and was glad the darkness hid it.

"You kin go home," Jed said, not glancing her way as he brought the saddle past.

"Are—are you sure? I feel like I should help." Or had she not done a proper job the last two times?

"I've got it tonight. Pa said so. It bein' late Friday night an' all." Jed flashed a smile as he came back to Kirby.

Friday night. The implications were obvious. Willow Hollow settled down a lot on the weekends, but outside Willow Hollow, a whole hullabaloo often occurred with bootleggers and the likes. Surely it was just because Pastor Stuart wanted her safe from them. But Widow Burman's judgmental face came to mind. As much as Lena would assure folks in Willow Hollow she was walking the straight and narrow the best she could, the shadow of Mom would follow her, tainting the very impressions she gave to folks.

"Okay." Lena stumbled a step away. "Thank you."

"'Night."

Lena didn't respond as she left the stables behind. A couple of houses had a slight glimmer through the shadowed windows. Late nighters who had candles lit, most likely. Lena had read about the electricity in modern cities—lights that were powerful enough to look like broad daylight at midnight. Mom had sung the praises of such inventions in the big city. Willow Hollow would be tickled pink to have such nonsense. But no one could afford it here. Oh, they were well-to-do compared to the mountain folk, but not that rich.

Lena slowed as she reached their shack. Sooner or later, Mom would notice she was getting back late and ask questions—unless she truly didn't care about Lena. Lena squared her shoulders and pulled open the screen door. She could feel the emptiness inside the dark house. That wasn't unusual.

"Mom?"

No answer.

Well, at least it would be one more day avoiding Mom's questions as to how she spent her days. Why Lena even thought the question would come was a lark. Mom wouldn't ask. Mom never asked. She just let Lena live her life while she lived hers. Except for *those* days. The days like last week. Next time that day came, Lena was prepared. She could counter each of Mom's accusations with proof of a paycheck. With reports of how she was worth something...

That day had just better wait about a month.

She lit a candle and brought it to the food shelves. A half jar of hard beans, three potatoes, rice, flour, the heel of a loaf of bread, and a couple of thin winter squash graced the shelves. She glanced at the stove. It was still as clean as she had left it yesterday. As soon as Mr. Armstrong handed her the first paycheck, she'd see what she could buy. Plenty of bread, for one. Then maybe some canned applesauce. Maybe even some of the fancy canned soup to make suppers easy. Because on nights like tonight, she wasn't going to bed up a fire just to eat. Coffee. Now that would be a marvel. She shivered, wishing for a cup to warm her now. But that was useless.

She grabbed the bread and took it with her to bed. She wrapped herself in the blanket and balled herself up. She'd be warm enough to fall asleep tonight and just dream about a day when she could afford a crackling fire to keep the room as warm as a summer day. She'd even be happy to share that warmth with Mom—Mom was always in a worse mood when the cold got to her.

A slight pang of guilt tripped her. She should know where Mom was, but she had no clue. There wasn't even a neighbor she could ask. Well, Widow Burman probably knew whether or not she got on the city-bound bus, but Lena wasn't that desperate. She'd be in Willow Hollow all day tomorrow and Sunday. Surely by then she'd see Mom.

She hadn't missed Mom. The realization made her throat go dry. She could get used to coming home with the house dark and lonely. It was better than bracing against Mom's accusations. How many paychecks would she have to save up before she could rent her own place? Sure, it would be cheaper just to stay here in the shack Mom's parents had bought for her. They didn't have rent—just grocery bills. But to Lena, it would be worth it to have a place of her own. Even if she had to eat nothing but beans every day. She just had to prove to Mr. Armstrong that this first week wasn't a failure. That she was capable of the job.

8

$\mathcal{J}$f it wasn't for Homer, Lena was pretty sure she wouldn't be able to face Mr. Armstrong today. She had avoided him in church yesterday—avoided everyone, really. Mom still hadn't been home and Lena didn't want to answer Pastor Stuart's kind questions and concerns. So she slipped into service as Mrs. Lee began the refrain for the first hymn and slipped out before the invitational hymn was finished, in order to avoid shaking Pastor Stuart's hand.

Since then, though, she had thought about the upcoming discussion with Mr. Armstrong. If he questioned last week's progress, she would ask him to wait and see how things progressed with Homer's help. And pray that maybe she could find another Homer for the other two routes.

The library was as dark as the night-time morning surrounding it. Of course, Mr. Armstrong wouldn't be here yet. It was only last Monday he had come in early to see Lena off. She was on her own. Not even the other two ladies who had their own routes were here yet. Lena had barely met Lillian Salisbury and Edna Sue O'Connell. They seemed to be nice enough ladies, but Lena was content to let them do their job while she did hers. That way, they wouldn't ask questions.

Relieved, Lena unlocked the Building and retrieved her sack from the library. She hadn't figured she needed to repack it on Saturday, given that she still had a large selection from last week's failure.

It was still dark when she left Willow Hollow, meaning it would be well past dawn by the time she crossed Franklin Creek and was at the houses. She had several hours to work up her courage to be friendly to those who had shunned her last week. *Lord, I need to do well here.* She had to succeed. To prove to Mom she was more than a lazy bum.

Unease fluttered through Lena's thoughts. Had it been three days or four that Mom hadn't been home? Should she have let someone know? Point them toward the Higgins' still? The city? She wasn't about to go search for Mom. Maybe, just maybe, Mom was actually out looking for another job. Lena gripped the saddle horn and leaned forward as Kirby tilted up with the terrain. Maybe she shouldn't doubt Mom's concern with finding another job so soon. But in the past, it had always been at least a week before Mom worked up the desire to find another job.

Determination suddenly filled Lena. She would keep this job, even if it meant facing down a crowd of frowning highlanders. She couldn't be like Mom, hopping from one job to the other, giving up when things got tough. She would just pray and keep moving forward, trusting that God would help her as she tried to help the needy.

The last few miles, Lena gave up trying to plan how to talk with these highlanders. Maybe she would just skip the first few houses and go to Homer's first. She tried to focus on the birds' music around her. It surrounded her, closing in on her just like the trees did on the narrow pathway. It was pleasant, really. It made her think of the Hundred Acre Wood. Maybe there were threats of heffalumps and woozles hiding somewhere nearby. She smiled at the thought. She should dig in the donations stack to see if there was a copy of A.A. Milne to give to the children. Maybe they would love it as much as she did.

Now, Kirby was easing his way up the steep, rocky slope that hugged the mountain on one side and gave way to treetops on the other. It wasn't too steep a drop-off, but it would still hurt if some mishap took place. Just a few more minutes and she'd be able to see the gray-brown of the first shack.

"I can do this." It was more of a breath than a whisper, but the words passing through Lena's lips instead of resting in her mind seemed to help. She sat up straighter as Kirby's balance leveled out. The first house appeared. This time, there was no boisterous woman calling out to her.

"Hello?" The word came out softer than the birds around her. Lena cleared her throat. "Hello! Good morning!" Still nothing. "I—I've brought you some books!" She nudged Kirby closer, not willing to leave the security of the saddle quite yet. "Okay, Kirbs, keep going."

She wasn't quite to the house that had the trio of women last time when a peal of laughter rang out—deep and hearty—followed by a sprinkling of children's giggles. Lena dismounted and walked past the house toward Homer's. His door was open, it being warmer today, and he was sitting on a wooden chair in the doorway. At least a dozen children were settled on the ground around him—the girls with sewing, the boys with whittling.

"'And now, for the third time Robin shot; but, alas for him! The arrow was ill-feathered, and, wavering to one side, it smote an inch outside the garland.'"

Some of the girls gasped and the boys chuckled.

"Robin *missed?*" One of the youngest leaned closer to Homer.

Homer looked up at the children and his eyes met Lena's.

"Well hello there! It's the book lady herself!"

The children all spun around, their eyes wide, but not as wary as last week.

She took a deep breath and plunged forward, determined to appear friendly. "Good morning, Homer. Children. When do you think Robin will discover it's the king disguising himself?" It was surprisingly easy to talk with them, eager over a story she had laughed at countless times.

"Oh," one of the taller girls said, "We already know. This is the second time Uncle Homer's read it to us."

Lena looked at Homer and he grinned.

"Well… I have more books here." She turned and opened her saddle pack. This time, the children came closer and made a semicircle around her.

"Here." Lena held out three books. They didn't have those shiny, new covers that would entice children of the city, but these children's eyes brightened because they knew the worth of the book as words on a page—not a shiny treasure to hoard. "Each of you may borrow one copy… if you'd like. If—if your parents give permission." Maybe if the children asked with Homer having laid the foundation of interest, the parents would be more likely to trust a townsperson from Willow Hollow.

"Wait a moment," Homer said. "Lemme get a blanket to spread so's you can all look and not get 'em dirty." He hurried inside and came out with a lap quilt that looked as if it had a hundred years of use. He carefully spread it on the ground then helped Lena put the books out.

"Why don't you all introduce yourselves before you just take up all Miss Book Lady's wares?"

Most of the children looked shyly at Lena, but a couple of the older ones volunteered their names. Rob, Marty, Phylis, Jack, Henry, Flora, Pollyanna, Ruby, Earl... the names rattled through Lena's mind as some of them tried to explain who was related to whom and how. She couldn't imagine life in a family with siblings—much less cousins and relatives all around her age. Seeing them joke and tease each other made her wonder if they really needed the world of books as much as she had growing up.

Finally, Homer helped the children settle on one book per family and repacked Lena's sack. "Now, scoot on home. We can't take up all of Miss Book Lady's time here." The children quickly obeyed, and Homer smiled at Lena.

"Come in for more tea?"

Lena hated to take more of their precious supply, but she didn't want to offend by rejecting it. "Thank you."

"Ya got any books that might interest Nora in there?" Homer called over his back as he led the way to the cabin.

"Of course! Yes sir." Lena untied the second sack. "What does she like?"

The happy sparkle in Homer's blue eyes faded just a little and he gave a sigh. "She'll like anything I read to her. We used to spend hours reading together. Talking 'bout what we read, ya know."

He opened his cabin door. "Nora, we've got company."

"Company?" There was a hint of delight in the older woman's voice. "Who is it?"

"It's our little book lady."

"Book lady? What does she do?"

"She brings books from the library to us here in the mountains."

Nora smiled at Lena. "How kind of you. Nice to meet you, Book Lady."

Lena bit back the reminder that they had met before when Homer gave his wife a patient smile.

"It's—it's nice to meet you as well."

"Now, about that there book," Homer said as he laid the sack on the table.

Lena dug until she found a copy of *Emma.* "Has she read Jane Austen?"

"Dunno that she has." Homer reached for the book and thumbed through it.

"Could you ask her?"

Homer gave Lena a sad smile. "Well…" He drawled the word out long enough to make Lena regret her question.

"It's okay. I didn't mean—"

"No, no." Homer sighed. He dropped his voice to a whisper. "You're gonna be here weekly. An' I'll have t' go an' introduce you every week 'cause she won't remember. Don't take it none too personal. She don't even remember her own kin."

Heat flooded through Lena. "I—I'm sorry." What could she say?

Homer smiled. "It's all right. God gave me a good memory, an' I can remember the good times we've done had. My Nora." Warmth flooded his tones. "She's the purdiest gal in these here mountains. Her hair silky blonde. Thoughtful too. You saw it last week—always offerin' our guests the best we got, no matter how poor we become. She's rich, my bride is."

Lena found herself blinking back tears.

"I have a question for you," Homer said.

Lena glanced up at him and smiled, hoping to hide her emotions. "Yes?"

"Can you get me a Bible? I'll done take right good care of it, and I'll be reading it to everyone in these mountains as much as I kin. Just havin' one to read every six months or so—that'd be a right fine blessing."

"I can ask." Did no one on this side of the mountain have a Bible? Lena thought of her own, safely tucked back home under her cot. When Pastor Stuart arrived in Willow Hollow, he made sure none of the homes went without a copy of God's Word. Since Mom didn't care about it, Lena claimed it as her own. She read it on occasion, but she knew without asking that if Homer had daily access to a Bible, he wouldn't give it just an occasional read. With that thought, Lena resolved to make a greater effort to be in her Bible.

She'd ask for Homer, all right. And if Pastor Stuart or Mr. Armstrong couldn't procure a copy, she'd give Homer her own. She had a job now, so she could save up to buy a new one. Until then, the passages she had memorized would keep her company.

9

$\mathcal{T}$oday had gone better than last Wednesday. The highlanders on her second route were less suspicious, even though they didn't take more than three books total. Still, Lena walked home with relief flooding through her. Mr. Armstrong still had said nothing about her job being on the line yesterday. Just maybe this would work out. Lena couldn't even begin to think of how marvelous it would be to have a steady income for *herself*. It seemed to be like the beginning of a Horatio Alger novel, where a character got a good break and had hope for a brighter future.

Dim light peeked through the screen door of the house. Lena's heart dropped and all the happy feelings of earlier dissipated. She should be glad Mom was home, but instead, she wanted to trek back to the library and spend the night amongst friends.

"Where ya been, girl?" Mom didn't wait until Lena was fully inside before posing her question. She sat at the table, her hair a picture in a magazine with its perfect waves and poof curls not quite reaching her shoulders. Even the candlelight flickering across her features made her almost look magazine-pretty.

Lena self-consciously pushed her drab brown hair over her shoulders as she groped for an answer. "Spending time with the library." It wasn't a lie. It just wasn't the whole truth.

Mom spat out a curse. "And here I am, trying to put food on the table, and you're doing nothing but wasting time with those wretched books."

"But I am—"

"Don't you sass me, girl." Mom stood. She was sober tonight, her poise tall and rigid. "When I was your age, I was forced to make a living on my own. And here I've done gone and raised a lazy bum."

"I'm not—"

"I'm not done talking!" Mom took a step closer—measured, exact, and perfect. Mom could have gone far in the world with her precision and attention to details—at least, when she was sober. She had the charm, the beauty, the poise. "The least you could do is cook while I'm out. But does Lena ever think of anyone besides herself? Ha!" Mom pointed a finger toward her. "Not since the day you were conceived. I spent weeks curled up on the couch sick because of you. And ever since you were born, you've been wanting nothing but my attention and what you can get from me. You're sixteen soon, girl. I've pampered you too long. As soon as your birthday's here, no more library. You'll find a fine city job that can clothe you without my help."

Mom spun on her heel, and her two-toned Oxfords pounded on the floor as she closed herself in her room.

"I… have a job." Lena mouthed the words to the candle. A job with the library—the very thing Mom demanded she leave. Lena blew out the candle before it wasted another centimeter. It was already only an inch tall, and there was no hint of replacing it soon. Lena sighed and put it on her mental list of things to buy to just survive without Mom providing for them. Already, her twenty-eight dollars was spent, and she hadn't seen a single greenback.

Next month, she'd be able to start saving. Maybe she could do without a food item or two. It wouldn't hurt to eat beans more frequently. Or to keep getting their one loaf of bread a week.

She went to bed without eating. Her stomach couldn't think about food when it was reeling from Mom's words. Did Mom think she couldn't remember? She knew Mom was sick her entire pregnancy. She knew Mom was rejected by her parents because she was with child. She knew why they were here at Willow Hollow instead of New York. Why did Mom have to keep reminding her?

She reached under the cot and pulled out *Little Women*. There was enough moonlight to read a chapter before she went to sleep. A dose of the March girls would lighten her heart to be able to sleep better. Except it didn't. She finished the chapter, and it was too dark to read further. She replaced the book with a sigh.

Her thoughts roamed up the mountain slopes to the huts that held poor highlanders. *I will lift up mine eyes unto the hills, from whence cometh my help…* It was God Who had made these hills—these mountains. God Who had painted such beauty around her. Yet right now, all she could feel was the ugliness of Mom's rejection. The bareness of life in this bare, cold shack. She did believe that God had provided this library job. In a sense, it was the hills themselves that provided this job and would help her free herself from Mom's clutches.

In essence, she knew that wasn't what the verse was speaking of—that it was the Creator of the hills Who helped. But tonight, her hope was anchored in what possibilities were linked with this mountaineer librarian job.

She wished she could have gone to prayer meeting. She didn't realize how much those midweek services uplifted her spirits, even when it was just a handful of them that met. But now, getting back late on Wednesdays thwarted that possibility. She thought back to her conversation with Homer on Monday. Something always seemed to be getting in the way of her being able to truly spend time with God and focus on reading the Bible. Moments like tonight, it wasn't the Bible she needed—it was an escape. An escape from reality. Even an escape from hoping things would change if she filled her mind with more of the Bible.

Her troubled thoughts drifted until she was asleep, but the sunbeams woke her with the same unsettled thoughts. She looked at Mom's door—a habit she had started when she was little. She could tell when Mom was awake or asleep. Something about the subtle movements that reverberated across their cold floor. This morning, she was still asleep.

Lena stood up and straightened her dress. A nightgown could go on her list, but that was a luxury, not a necessity. She stirred the fire. The coals were still warm. Remembering

Mom's words about cooking last night, she scrubbed two potatoes then placed them in the oven. They'd be ready by lunchtime. She placed a pan on the stove and filled it with water. She'd leave some oatmeal for Mom to eat when she woke up. But if Lena planned it right, she'd eat and be gone before Mom stirred.

Running her fingers through her hair, Lena grabbed her Bible and *Little Women*. She'd spend a few minutes in the Psalms then continue Jo's journey. Jo was keeping a secret much like Lena was—making money without her parents' knowledge. Granted, it would take a quarter of a year before Lena made close to the hundred dollars that Jo did with her one manuscript, but that was a different era.

This morning, Lena was in Psalm 136. Her eyes rested on verse one: "O give thanks unto the LORD; for He is good: for His mercy endureth for ever." Lena stopped to check the oatmeal. It was nearly done. "O give thanks unto the God of gods: for His mercy endureth for ever. O give thanks to the Lord of lords: for His mercy endureth for ever."

She scooped out half the oatmeal into the metal cup that served as a bowl. She had gotten used to eating her oatmeal without cream and sugar. She suspected Mom still had a stash of sugar kept away for it, but it would be fruitless to ask. "To Him which led His people through the wilderness: for His mercy endureth for ever."

Lena paused over those words. *Father God in heaven, I surely feel like I'm in a wilderness right now.* Goodness, she had been wandering in the wilderness forty years already, and her sixteenth birthday wasn't even here. *I know that You led the children of Israel faithfully through the wilderness and saw them through with all their complaining and moaning. I need You to see me through.* Did the children of Israel know how many years it would be when they began wandering? Did they count down the days? Lena wasn't sure. But if they could last forty years, surely she could last a few months until she could get out on her own—that was definitely a Promised Land to look forward to.

She finished the Psalm about the time she finished breakfast, washed the cup, and headed outside. Today she'd find Pastor Stuart and ask about Homer's Bible. She'd talk with Mr. Armstrong about the progress she'd made on her second route. Anything to keep her from being home all day with Mom.

10

$\mathcal{M}$om came to church with her on Sunday. Lena pasted on a smile that was just as artificial as Mom's. She had said she had a new job—at least, she had been in the city each day and was drinking less and curling her hair more. She hadn't said anything more to Lena about being a lazy bum. Those should be good signs. But there was no rejoicing in Lena's heart as they entered the church—five minutes late, of course. The heavy scent of lavender mixed with lemon and bergamot assaulted Lena's senses. The perfume was too expensive for Mom—it probably cost the price of a full month of food. But Lena couldn't voice these thoughts. She'd just smile and pretend everything was going just dandy at home.

The hymn helped some. Lena couldn't really sing "Happy in the Savior" and not be uplifted with the lyrics and the movement of the other voices while she held onto the lead note with several other women. Mom didn't sing. She moved her lips, but Lena knew it was just as much a facade as coming to church.

Amanda Tero

Pastor Stuart got up to preach and announced Ephesians chapter four. He had been going through Ephesians for several months now. They were in the last few verses. Lena flipped the pages until she found the twenty-sixth verse. "Be ye angry, and sin not: let not the sun go down upon your wrath: Neither give place to the devil."

Pastor paused for a moment and Lena thought on the verses she had just read. She wasn't angry. Not really. Upset, yes. That was the natural human response.

"Let him that stole steal no more:" Pastor Stuart continued to verse twenty-eight, "but rather let him labour, working with his hands the thing which is good, that he may have to give to him that needeth."

Lena felt Mom shift as she leaned over and pointed the verse out. Her manicured nail tapped the word "labour" as she whispered, "You better be listening today."

A weight settled in Lena's stomach, and she clenched her teeth to hold back the tears. It was wicked sinful to wish that someone wasn't in church, but, just now, she wished Mom wasn't. She didn't hear another word of the sermon.

They filed out in order, and when they reached Pastor Stuart, Mom offered a gracious hand. "Lovely sermon this morning, as always, Pastor."

Pastor Stuart's round face kept that genuine, ready smile. "Thank you, ma'am, but all glory to the Lord. I've heard you found another job in the city."

"I did. It's truly a blessing in such a time of need. I've been talking with Lena about her getting a job. I think it's high time she learns the principles you were preaching about—working with her own hands."

74

Lena felt heat creep into her face until she was sure it would burst from all the blood that was in it. Pastor Stuart knew she was working at the library. She wasn't ready for Mom to know yet.

"I think Lena is doing a fine job down that path, ma'am." He turned and offered Lena his hand.

She should tell him "Thank you," but that might lead him to continue the conversation about her job. So instead, she blurted out the first thing she could think of, "I was wondering if there were some extra Bibles in the missionary box?" She held back a wince. It was still pertaining to her job.

Pastor's smile broadened. "I love questions like that, Lena. Come by my home after lunch. Is this for one of—"

"Yes, sir." It was rude to interrupt, but Mom was still there. She wasn't really listening, Lena could tell, but at any moment, she could snap her focus back to Lena and Pastor and then the questions would come. Not like Lena was trying to hide anything—it wasn't something bad she was doing, after all. "Thank you, Pastor. I'll be by."

Lena stepped away and let Pastor Stuart turn to those behind her. She walked beside Mom in silence, nodding and smiling to the townspeople they passed on the street to their home.

As soon as the door closed behind them, Mom removed her hat and smoothed a hand over her flawless hair. "What was that holy garble you and the Pastor were having? Don't you already have a Bible?"

Lena's heart sank with the questions. "It's—it's for a friend."

Mom rolled her eyes. "How sweet of you, to be offering spiritual guidance to a friend. It's not going to do your thick brain any good." She opened the door to her room. "I need a quick wink before lunch. Wake me when it's ready."

Lena changed from her Sunday dress to everyday clothes before she dared to touch food. Trust Mom to ruin a good sermon. Lena couldn't remember anything but the delicate angle of Mom's finger as she pointed out that verse. Last night, she was so close to telling Mom about her job. Today, that was the last thing she wanted to do. She just knew that somehow Mom would find a way to make the library job a disappointment instead of the biggest thing that had ever happened in Lena's life.

Lena ate her lunch as she was preparing Mom's then left Mom to eat alone while she went to Pastor Stuart's. Usually she didn't mind sticking around Pastor's. His children had always been nice to Lena—especially friendly little Mary. And then there was Lillian who was staying with the Stuarts while she worked at the library. She was friendly, but Lena was hesitant to make any friendship.

Today she just wanted to get the Bible and then find a place to curl up and finish *Little Women*. Mr. Armstrong had let her borrow *Little Men* at the same time. She was sure she could read both of them today.

The Stuart home didn't take long to reach. Lena walked to the front door and knocked. It swung open, and bright-eyed Mary was there. "Pa said you'd be along. Said to bring ya to him in his study." Her pudgy hand slipped into Lena's, and she marched to a closet of a room that served as Pastor Stuart's study. Lena hadn't been there before. The window was framed by bookshelves and a desk sat under it. There were two wooden chairs. Not much room for more, but Lena figured it was a right fine place for a pastor to do his studying.

"I'm glad you came," Pastor Stuart said. He motioned toward a chair, and Lena sat down. "Now, about this Bible…"

"Homer asked for it." When Pastor raised his eyebrows, Lena realized he probably didn't know Homer—he probably never came to Willow Hollow. "He's an elderly man that I bring books to on Mondays. He asked for a Bible."

Pastor smiled and walked to his bookcase. "I do have a copy he can have."

"Have?" Homer was going to be overjoyed.

"Yes. I know these mountain folk can't afford to buy it, so it's one of the ways I want to bless them as I know of their need."

"Thank you, Sir." Lena took the Bible from him. It was one of the larger copies. Her hands couldn't quite fit all the way around it—unlike her small one that could be easily carried everywhere.

She turned to go, but Pastor laid his hand gently on her shoulder. "You know if you need help—with anything—Lena, you can trust Mrs. Stuart and me."

Heat flooded to her face, and she didn't turn to look at him. "Yes, sir… I—I know." What would Mom say if she knew Lena divulged family information to the pastor of their community? The thought made Lena go resolute. She straightened her shoulder and gave Pastor her practiced smile. "Have a good afternoon."

As soon as she was back outside, Lena clutched the big Bible to her chest. Her heart pounded against it wildly. What was it that Pastor was suspecting? If he knew the full truth of the matters, would he be so congenial? Lena hurried home. Everything was going to be all right. She was going to bury herself in Jo's world and forget that Mom hated her. Forget about Mom's finger pointing accusingly at the verse. Forget that Pastor could detect something was awry. And tomorrow, she would be back to her normal self, alone on the mountains as the Book Lady.

11

*J*t was good to see true delight in another's eyes because of something she did. Lena could erase all of the worries of yesterday when she saw Homer's overjoyed face. He reverently thumbed through the pages of his Bible, still not believing it was his to keep. She wasn't sure, but she thought she could detect tears in his eyes as well.

"I want to meet your pastor someday," he finally said. "I don't get out to Willow Hollow anymore. These old bones can't make it." His eyes twinkled at Lena as he spoke. He didn't seem that old. She suspected it was more Nora's health that kept him back than his own.

"Tell me, Miss," Homer placed the Bible on the table and laid his hand on it as he leaned forward, "what did Pastor preach yesterday?"

In a rush, it was all back. Mom's finger. Her accusatory whisper. Her disapproval in front of the pastor. Lena pasted a smile. "He preached on Ephesians 4." She scrambled thoughts in her mind, but all she could see was that one word burning in her mind: labor, labor, labor… It hissed in her mind as Mom's voice, blocking out anything else Pastor Stuart had said.

Lena realized Homer was still there, waiting. "He preached on work and how it's good for us."

Homer gave her a gentle smile. She looked down.

"Is something wrong?"

Lena shook her head. She couldn't trust her voice.

"Ya don't have to pretend with me, Honey. God knows, we all got our sadnesses in life. I'd be right honored if you felt you could just tell me what's on your heart."

Lena clenched her hands around the jar of tea Homer had insisted she drink. She lifted it to her lips and pretended to take a sip. She couldn't swallow anything right now, but the warm liquid moistened her lips.

Homer's fingers tapped the Bible gently. He cleared his throat as if to change the subject. "If ya don't mind me asking, why did you decide to become our Book Lady?"

That question wasn't any better. But Homer didn't know.

"I—I love books." That was a solid start. Solid truth. "Mr. Armstrong—he's our librarian—said there were openings in the library. I needed the money. It was a good fit." A heavenly solution, if she thought on it. An excuse to be away from Mom and out of the shack that seemed smaller everyday she had to spend imprisoned in it. Lena lifted the jar to her lips and took a real drink this time.

"Ah." Homer nodded. "And your parents, what do they do?"

Lena's throat restricted, and the tea half-drowned her. She choked before she could help herself. "Sorry."

Homer waited until she stopped coughing, his blue eyes patient.

"Uh… my mom works in the city. I—I…" Why had she thought she'd be able to leave her life down in Willow Hollow? What would Homer think of her family situation?

Homer seemed to fill in the blank. "I'm sorry for your loss." Only, he didn't fill in the blank correctly.

She'd have to let him believe incorrectly. The dark smudge on her family should be left in Willow Hollow.

That thought followed her as she continued along the trail, collecting last week's books and presenting new books. Now that Homer had gone with her twice, she was able to continue this trail without the rejection and suspicion that still laced the other two routes.

She was getting used to the dark nights coming back to Willow Hollow. The streets weren't quite cleared of people tonight, so it must not be as late as it had been the other nights. Lena dismounted in front of the Building. It was still unlocked, and a few people still milled inside, their voices low. They stopped talking altogether and just watched as Lena entered the door. She felt her face grow hot. She hid it by ducking her head and hurrying to the room that held the library. It was unlocked as well.

"Good evening, Lena," Mr. Armstrong greeted her.

"Evening." Lena could breathe easier in here, a place where she was embraced and accepted by others. The books, mainly. They didn't cast accusing glares at her. Of course, Mr. Armstrong didn't either. Well, except tonight.

"You've gotten in late every night, Lena. How far up are you going?"

"Oh…" Lena shrugged. "I just go until dusk." The way she figured it, the further up she went, the more books she was able to distribute, and the better she did her job, the more likely she was to keep her job.

Mr. Armstrong released a sigh as he took the saddle pack from Lena. "You don't have to try so hard."

Lena's eyes widened, and she looked at him without meaning to.

He gave her a grin. "My dear, you're not the only traveling librarian we have. Miss O'Connell and Miss Salisbury are on route also."

"But I'm the only one with my route." Hesitancy filled Lena as soon as she said it. "Right?"

"Yes, you are. But you can't get back this late."

There it was again. Another person suspicious of her nighttime behavior. All because of Mom's past.

"That is," Mr. Armstrong rushed to finish, "you're working more hours than we agreed upon. You don't have to put in twelve hours a day. Or fourteen."

Lena hadn't calculated how many hours she'd been out on the mountains. But, this didn't sound like Mr. Armstrong was firing her from the job. Maybe it was just another part of the process of a trial run. This was an angle she hadn't considered. She'd do her best to please Mr. Armstrong. If she pleased him, she had a better likelihood of keeping her job. "When do you want me to head down?" She tried to keep her tone polite instead of timid, but it came out squeaky.

"Maybe head back by four o'clock?"

She didn't have a watch. She tried to calculate how the sun might appear that late in the afternoon.

"Or… try to be back in Willow Hollow by dusk."

That helped some. Lena nodded her head. "Yes sir. I will try my best." Try? That didn't sound like someone confident in their work. "I mean, I'll do it." She made herself look Mr. Armstrong in the eyes and found him smiling at her, as always.

"Now that we have that covered, what book do you want tonight?"

Lena couldn't help but smile back. Of course he'd know she'd be hankering for something as soon as she was able. She had left *Little Women* and *Little Men* on his desk this morning when she left.

"Does something like this seem to your liking?" Mr. Armstrong reached under his desk and pulled out a green book, its cover etched with flowers.

"The third book!" Lena leaped forward and grabbed the book by Martha Finley, hugging it to her heart. Mr. Armstrong's smile only got bigger. She'd seen him overly excited about a book as well. "May I borrow all three? It's been a year since I've read the first two."

"Yes, my dear. I've already got them reserved for you." He pulled out the first two volumes of *Mildred Keith* and handed them over. "Just don't stay up too late reading them. I could use a hand here at the library for a few hours tomorrow—plus you need to pack your sack." His voice had a teasing lilt to it.

"I'll be here." She waved as she backed out of the library. The hands on the clock over Mr. Armstrong's desk informed her that it was past closing time, so she couldn't linger here where oil lamps made it light enough to read. Nor would she dare stick around in the great room of the Building where other people could see her and talk about her behind feigned secrecy. She'd just have to wait until tomorrow to dive into Mildred's story again, reliving the life of a girl who served her family through illness and turmoil. Once again, Lena vowed to buy candles as soon as she had a paycheck.

12

*T*here had been no supper last night. Lena walked through the drizzly cold weather. Mom had woken up more irritable today, catching Lena before she could escape to the library. And now Lena had to run to the store to beg Mr. Clark for more groceries. She pulled her coat around her. If only it could keep her from the prying eyes of the townspeople in addition to giving her warmth. Mom, who loved the big city with its excitement and people, wouldn't understand the qualms Lena had entering this tiny general store. But then, she also didn't have any qualms about what others said behind her back.

The store's bell jostled, defying the gloominess of the morning surrounding her.

"Good morning!" The exuberant greeting seemed to match the bell. Mr. Clark was jolly, as usual. This poor store needed a drop of joviality. It was almost darker inside than outside. A crowd of six or so men hung around the stove in the middle—the stove that was more for warmth than light, as its windows were tinted gray from the smoke. "What can I get you, Lena?"

Lena walked past the crowd in the middle and handed over her basket and the list she had made while Mom was babbling this morning.

"One moment, please."

Lena took a step to the side, bringing her closer to the exterior wall and further from the men in the middle. They had seemed to ignore her, much like everyone in town did.

The bell jingled and Widow Burman stepped in.

Or almost everyone in town. Lena turned to focus her attention on something else. Too late, she realized she was staring at Mr. Clark's assortment of tobaccos and cigarettes.

"Those are the devil's own work, those things."

Lena turned to face Widow Burman. "Yes, ma'am." She tried to sound agreeable, but she was afraid all that came out was fear.

Widow Burman didn't give any greeting or smile. She just looked Lena over—head to toe. Lena tried to be sure she didn't wiggle under the scrutiny, but her toes tingled something fierce. "H-how do you do today, Mrs. Burman?"

Widow Burman sniffed. "Bones hurting with this cold, wet weather. I see you're in town today—not wandering around on the mountains doing God-knows-what. He's watching you, girl, you know that, right?"

More than embarrassment flooded through Lena. The heat was exploding on her face—she knew it. "I—" The words stopped coming out and Widow Burman's eyebrows rose.

"I know you come to church. But what you do during the week is just as important as what you do on Sunday."

A dozen responses flooded through Lena's mind, but all she could manage was a weak, "Yes ma'am."

Mr. Clark came back to the counter. Lena turned, grateful to have a reason to turn her back on Widow Burman.

"Thank you," Lena said as she took the handles of the basket.

"Um, Lena…" Mr. Clark lowered his voice. He glanced around and Lena knew Widow Burman was nearby. "I wanted to show you this new product we have that may interest your mother." He motioned for Lena to follow.

Her heart sank as they walked toward the back of the store. There were new products there, all right, but those weren't what Mr. Clark was singling her out for. Mom had never bought the low-grade beauty products that Mr. Clark's General Store offered. She preferred the rich quality of things in the city.

"Your tab has gotten too high. I really shouldn't let you bring these groceries home without accepting payment." Mr. Clark's voice was low and somehow still held a cheerful tone.

"I'm sorry…" Lena glanced at the contents in the basket. They were all necessities. Food. Something they couldn't live without. "I'll ask Mom about it. She just got a new job." She looked up at Mr. Clark, hoping her expression was apologetic. She wasn't apologetic though—she was downright mortified. How could Mom spend dozens of dollars on makeup and hair product and rack up the bills in a struggling mountain store? Unless... Lena hoped that the stores in the city weren't hounding Mom for the same thing. "Here, I'm sure we don't need all of this." She dug through the basket and pulled out a can of milk and half of the eggs. She'd just go without the next week.

Mr. Clark patted her on the shoulder. She forced herself not to cringe away from it. "Go ahead, take it all. But I really need you to make a payment on your tab before purchasing more groceries."

Lena blew out the air she didn't realize she was holding. "I really appreciate it, Mr. Clark." She rushed out the door before she could really register his reply—which was probably a cheerful "No problem" or "Don't worry about it." She should be counting her blessings that it was Mr. Clark and not Mrs. Clark who had served her today. It would be Lena's luck to get Mrs. Clark on one of her moody days rather than cheerful days.

The grayish-blue bus roared to life down the road, holding all the city workers and Mom. A few children played in tiny puddles as Lena walked through the cluster of shacks to the one she and Mom shared. She had given up trying to make friends with the neighbors a long time ago, when she realized how their tongues wagged about her and Mom.

She hurried up the steps and into the house. She set the basket down then brushed off the water droplets that were just waiting to soak her coat through. Movement in the kitchen area made her stop.

"Mom? But—didn't the bus—I thought..."

"I hope you got something decent to eat. The food shelf's empty."

Lena walked stiffly as she brought the basket to Mom. It was one thing to tell Mr. Clark she'd talk to Mom about their bill. Quite another to actually follow through.

Mom muttered under her breath as she dug through the contents. "Didn't I say something about hot cocoa?"

"Mr. Clark doesn't carry cocoa." Or, she didn't think he did. It was too expensive an item for Willow Hollow folk to indulge on.

"I don't see half the things I listed this morning."

Lena glanced down at the paper in the basket. "I wrote it down as you were—"

"Stop sassing me. I guess I just need to go next time."

I wish you would. Lena bit off the words before they escaped. She waited as Mom finished unloading the groceries onto their makeshift table. "Uh…" She didn't know how to start.

Mom gave her an impatient look. It was then Lena noticed… her hair wasn't swept up in perfection. Her clothes hadn't been pressed this morning. Her face not made up.

"Well?" Mom shifted and placed a hand on her hip. "Speak up."

There was only one way to get over with this. Lena let the words rush out like a swollen mountain stream. "Our tab's too full. We have to pay him before we get more groceries."

Mom threw her hands in the air then let them fall to her sides. A can of milk crashed to the floor. "What do you expect me to do about that?"

Lena took a step backward.

"It's this wretched depression. No one's hiring."

No one but the library. A dry heat rushed over Lena. She couldn't see Mom—with her finesse and style—trekking miles each day on horseback in order to meet grimy mountain folk who rejected the very blessing the librarians were trying to bestow. No, it wasn't even worth mentioning it to Mom. But if Mom found out she had a job…

"I've tried. You've seen me. I've gotten up every day—or no," Mom interrupted herself, "You haven't seen me. Exactly what do you spend your days doing?"

"I told you—with the lib—"

"Don't sass me, girl. I know the library isn't open each day."

Did she? Lena took another step backwards.

"Don't you dare dart away from me, Lena Rose. You're going to answer my question."

"Why do you even care?" The words exploded from Lena, wrenching from her heart. "You never tell me where you are."

Mom stepped forward but Lena darted away before she could grip her arm. "I'm your *mother*. I should know what my daughter is up to."

"You've never asked before."

"But I'm asking now."

Lena wished she was as fast a thinker as Jo in *Little Women.* Either that, or have planned out her response.

"Lena. What have you been doing?" Mom's voice was hard as ice.

Why she cared now, Lena didn't know. But the way Mom was hovering only meant that if she didn't get an answer, Lena would get a bruise.

"I'm bringing books to the mountains." Lena hoped that was enough of an explanation.

Understanding flashed through Mom's dark eyes. That only scared Lena more. "A library job, huh?" A self-satisfied smile grew on Mom's face and she stood straight, folding her arms. "You thought you could hide it from me—when there are those in town concerned about you?"

Widow Burman. It had to have been her. Lena shrugged. "I wasn't trying to hide it."

"Oh yes you were. Don't lie to me." The casual poise Mom had obtained melted into determination. "Just what were you thinking about doing with those paychecks?"

"I—I…" Heat buzzed around Lena's head. She couldn't tell Mom that she was planning on ultimately running away.

"You had plans. I knew it. I need to have a chat with Curt." Mom grabbed her wool coat from the peg by the door. "You're too young to be entrusted with money."

"Wait! Mom." Lena rushed forward and grabbed Mom's arm before she thrust it into the coat sleeve. "I was going to help pay for groceries." With some of the money. Just because she had no choice—she had to eat. And Mr. Clark wouldn't allow them to buy more food until he was paid.

"You're under-age."

"What were you doing at my age?"

Mom froze and Lena released her arm. Lena's throat ached, and the heat that swarmed around her turned to ice. "I didn't—I…"

Mom would never un-hear the words now.

"That was different." Mom's words were dangerously measured—that perfect volume right above a whisper, yet

91

screamed in its subdued tones. "My parents could afford me."

She jerked her coat on and charged out the door.

Lena rushed to the door before it slammed shut, ready to follow Mom. But Mom wasn't heading toward the streets of Willow Hollow. Her steps traced the path that Lena knew led to the Higgins. Tears stung Lena's eyes. She didn't know which was worse: Mom running to Mr. Armstrong or downing more of the Higgins' moonshine. Both of them brought problems Lena wasn't willing to face.

13

Lena was at the library well before the sun had thought about peeking over the mountaintops and gracing Willow Hollow with its beams. She was here even before Widow Burman would be up and about—unless that wretched woman never slept.

Her fingers fumbled with the keys. What did it matter? She'd just as soon not have a job if Mom was going to take control of the funds. The door opened, and Lena stepped inside. They'd had a new book shipment in yesterday, and she had gone through them eagerly, leaving enough for Lillian and Edna to bring on their routes as well.

She saddled Kirby and attached the saddle pack. She'd feel sorry for the horse except that Kirby seemed almost more eager to get on the trail than she did. She mounted and settled into the saddle before urging Kirby forward. She didn't even have to direct him out of town now. He had learned his route. They took the path southward. Franklin Creek reflected the moonlight up ahead. Kirby splashed across the shallow creek and stepped back onto dry land.

Here the path became rockier and began its steep ascent. Lena leaned forward as Kirby tread upward. The sun was now beginning to change the shade of the sky above them. Birds began their wake-up calls.

Lena pulled back on the reins as they neared the crossway. Today's route was straight ahead—Monday's route to the left, and Friday's route to the right. She looked at the three different trails. Though the mountain morning was peaceful, the argument with Mom last night roared in her mind.

She pulled on the reins and directed Kirby to the left. Mr. Armstrong might not appreciate her deviating from her route, but he wouldn't have to know. She balanced as Kirby went down one slope then up another.

The plans she had made these past weeks while riding the trails fluttered through her mind only to be torn away and burned up by Mom's greed. She had spent the rest of the evening away. Lena tried not to blame the Higgins, but she knew better than to hope that Mom thought about the grocery bill rather than her insatiable thirst for their corn liquor.

Dawn touched the sky as Lena neared the first cabin. The boisterous woman—whom Lena learned was called Melba Foster—was waking her children up. Some scent filtered through from her cabin, but Lena couldn't discern what mix of berries it was. She dismounted and took Kirby's reins. It was too early for anyone to be out of their cabins, and that suited Lena just fine.

She stopped in front of Homer and Nora's cabin. The door was shut. She wanted to knock on the door, but just as much didn't want to bother them.

Why was she here?

She glanced around. No one was nearby. No one needed to know she was here. She led Kirby down the trail and tied him to a nearby tree and dug in the saddle pack. The folks up here wouldn't be ready for new books after only two days. It was foolish to come here.

But now that she was here… She pulled out a hardback copy of *The Black Arrow* and stared at it for a few seconds. She'd not read this one yet. She patted Kirby in farewell.

With her back to Homer's cabin, she hurried down the slope, hiding herself in the depths of the trees and shrubbery. She finally reached a place where the ground leveled at the base of a tree. Perfect. She slid to the ground and curled herself in a ball.

On a certain afternoon, in the late springtime, the bell upon Tunstall Moat House was heard ringing at an unaccustomed hour…

It didn't take long for Lena to be lost in Dick's story and the questions of Sir Daniel's alliance. She traveled through the woods as Dick discovered his father was murdered. And, now that Dick knew of it, his own life was endangered. And John Matcham was really not—

"Lena?"

Lena jumped and clutched the book to her chest.

"Oh, Homer." Instead of relief, Lena felt dread as Homer tilted his head to read the book's title.

"Ya came all the way up here to read?"

Warmth attacked Lena's face. "Well—not… exactly…" She didn't have any plans when she came up here. She just needed an escape.

95

"Ah, Robert Louis Stevenson. A great writer."

"I haven't read this one yet." It seemed as if Lena was shying away from her duty as a horseback librarian. She wasn't—exactly. Just... realigning her schedule. "I wasn't hiding out here. Not really. It just... it's so peaceful out here." She looked away from Homer. Though it was mid-winter, there were enough pine trees to cloak the mountain in a green canopy.

"Peaceful—compared against...?" He seemed to read straight through her.

Lena bit her lower lip as Homer held his hand out to her and helped her to her feet.

"Willow Hollow," she blurted out. "It's a small town, but it's still a town."

The left side of Homer's mouth lifted and he chuckled as he shook his head. "Come in for some breakfast?"

"Oh, I couldn't." Yet, as she said it, she noticed the pain gnawing in her stomach. She had gone to bed without eating last night—her whole being was too much in turmoil to stomach food.

"Come on." Homer walked in front of her, using a walking stick to help him up the slope. "Your horse decided he was bored and got to nosing around my place." He glanced back to grin at Lena. "Don't worry, I tied him good this time."

That tattletale. So it was his fault Lena's silence was disturbed.

When they reached the house, Homer stepped inside first. "We got company, Nora."

Nora looked up with a smile. "Why, hello there." She held out a shaky hand to Lena. "What's your name?"

It had only been two days this time. Lena wanted to step away from Nora, but at Homer's insistence, she took the step forward to clasp the lady's hand in her own. It was cold and weak.

"This here's our little Book Lady. Remember the book we've been reading?"

"Oh... oh, yes..." Nora gave Lena another smile, but beneath that smile, Lena detected a hint of confusion.

"Are you hungry?" Homer asked, bending over to plant a kiss on his wife's cheek.

"I guess so, if you think I should be."

Homer patted Nora's shoulder. "I'll fix us some nice scrambled eggs. Little Henry brought them over."

"And which one's Henry?"

"Ruth's youngest."

"Oh..." Nora shifted in her chair. "That's right."

"So tell me, Lena," Homer walked to the stove and fed the fire, "Do ya find *The Black Arrow* and *Robin Hood* to be similar or different?"

Lena thumbed through the pages of her book. "I think... *Robin Hood* has more humor. There is humor in *The Black Arrow*, but it feels more action-packed. And it has more of a theme rather than a collection of events, like *Robin Hood*." Just so long as he didn't ask which one she liked better. Comparing books was like comparing... flowers. They were all wonderful in their own sense.

The gentle sizzling of eggs filled the silence. Homer divided them between three plates. "Breakfast's ready."

Lena watched as Nora scooted herself forward in her chair. One hand clutched the arm of the chair and the other the head of the wooden cane. After two rocking movements, Nora pulled herself to her feet. Her walk to the table was slow, but she made it by the time Homer brought the food to the table.

"Father, I thank You for providing this food for us."

Lena quickly bowed her head and squeezed her eyes shut.

"You're always so good to see to our every need. Thank you for the way Ruth, Helen, and Anna watch out for us. Bless them and their families. Draw us closer to You. Forgive me where I've sinned against You. In Jesus' Name, Amen."

Nora echoed the "amen" and picked up her fork.

Breakfast was filled with light chatter about books. Nora didn't offer much to the conversation, but kept looking between Homer and Lena, following along. Finally, Nora pushed her plate away.

"Finished already?" Homer raised his bushy white eyebrows. "Honey, you've only eaten a few bites."

Nora shrugged. "I'm finished."

"Here, let's get you another—"

"No!" Nora pushed the plate further from her.

Lena slid back in her chair and she watched the interchange.

"Would ya like a biscuit?"

"Nope." Nora huffed and shook her head. "I told you, I'm done. That means done." She stood up and slowly walked back to her chair.

Homer's eyes followed her. They glistened as he turned back to Lena. "That gal sure could cook when she had the mind to do it. She could make even a stuffed man want to eat another full course. One bite of her spiced apple cake—whoo. Honey, you ain't had nothin' if you ain't had Nora's cooking." He took another bite of his eggs. "I wished you'd have known Nora when she was herself. Never a bad word to anyone, my bride. She's just not herself anymore."

Lena let Homer talk. How a man could look past the blatant defiance just now and recall only the good memories, she couldn't understand. Anytime she looked at Mom, she saw Mom for who she was today—ungrateful, controlling, vain.

"Helen's asked me about looking into one of those special hospitals to help Nora's memory. Even if I could afford it, it'd do more harm than good. Nora ain't herself, even more when we visit the gals' place. I can't take her down the mountains for special care. No matter how hard it is to see her lose her bearings here, it'd be that much harder when Nora's in a place she don't know herself."

Lena nodded. She hadn't thought about it, really. She'd only really been around one older woman, Aunt Melba Lynn, and she was sound in mind until the day she passed.

"It's hard—seeing the one you love most suffer. But sometimes you've just got to do what's best for them." Homer shook himself as if he was returning from another world. "Sorry for that ramble."

"It's all right." Lena stood and gathered the plates. "Would you like me to help with the dishes?"

"Now, I won't be one to reject help when it's offered." Homer took Nora's plate with the leftover eggs and finished them himself. "If you've a mind to, you can wash up the dishes while I get everything else cleaned."

Lena plunged the dishes into the washbasin that already had water in it. Homer kept a clean place; it wouldn't be long before she was done and could return to Dickie's adventures, living through his problems rather than her own.

She finished drying the last dish and placed it on the shelf with the others. Homer was at the table. He had *The Black Arrow* opened and was skimming the first page. He looked up with a sheepish grin. "I can see why you didn't hear me walking up. But I do have a question for you."

"Yes sir?" Lena hung the towel on the peg above the washbasin.

"What're ya really hiding from up here?"

14

She wasn't hiding. But why did her heart race and her knees feel weak?

"Forgive me if that's too personal." Homer's light blue eyes were filled with concern. "You don't seem very happy, Lena."

When did he stop calling her by "Book Lady?" She much preferred it over her given name. She took a deep breath and sat down in the chair that was still pulled out from breakfast. Her fingernail traced the wood grain of the table.

"Mom won't let me keep the money I rightfully make." She didn't attempt to hide the bitterness that seeped in. "She—uh—she's only going to waste it."

She waited for Homer to say something, but instead, he chose silence.

Lena shrugged. She didn't want to say anything else.

"Well," he finally talked, drawing the word out for a few seconds. "Maybe your ma knows what's best."

"It's not that!" Lena fisted her hand. "She doesn't know what's best. She'll spend the money on liquor and beauty. I know it."

Fire crackled in the stove.

"It doesn't matter what I say." Lena's voice sounded hollow, even to herself.

How could Lena know what was good for the family, when it was her conception that had brought them to the poverty of Willow Hollow in the first place? Why would Mom even listen to her? If she had only been born to someone else—to someone who would have actually cared they had a daughter. To someone like Homer and Nora.

"I was going to help pay for food—I *was*."

Now, they'd be eating the same thing as always. Scrounging around with the bare minimum when this paycheck could at least allow them to get some meat once in a while. Sure, Lena had a long list of other things to buy, but she wasn't going to be Mom and waste paycheck after paycheck. She had a plan.

"The one chance I get to prove to Mom that I can do something—and she steals it away."

Moisture tickled Lena's cheeks. She brushed the tears away impatiently with her hand and finally looked at Homer. He was still quietly waiting.

"I—I... didn't mean to say all that." She took a shuddering breath, but it didn't make anything feel better. Instead, her problems only weighed on her more heavily.

"Honey, I'm always here to listen."

That did it. Lena leaned forward and buried her face in her arms. She wasn't going to let herself sob—not here—but the tears poured from her eyes. Why couldn't Mom ever once listen? Wouldn't that change things? Instead, she interrupted. She dominated every conversation. She ignored Lena's thoughts and concerns on every matter. And when Lena finally did what Mom had been hounding her to do, she took control of the paycheck.

"It's more than the money, ain't it?" Homer asked gently. He still hadn't moved from where he stood.

Lena swallowed until her throat loosened from its tension. Finally, she looked up. She probably looked horrible—she hadn't brushed her hair this morning more than running her fingers through it, and now her face would be splotchy from crying. Mom hated it when she looked this way.

She would also hate it if she knew Lena was here blabbering their life's story to an old mountain man. Or would she even care?

Homer was right. It didn't involve money. Things were so confusing with Mom right now.

Still, Homer waited. He wasn't going to make her tell him anything. It wasn't the way of mountain folk. But he genuinely cared. He had helped Lena get to her feet here in this route. He always invited her in to share a glass of tea. And the way he loved his wife when she was so different from the woman he had married…

Lena took a deep breath and brought her hands down into her lap. Her fingers toyed with a loose thread from her dress. "I… don't know my father." It was the first time she had really told anyone. Oh, people assumed. They probably knew. But it wasn't something spoken of. "Mom was sent to Willow Hollow when she was expecting me. Lived with Great-Aunt Melba Lynn until she passed on. I don't have any family." She swallowed. It was easier to speak of the past than of the present, but it was the present she was facing today. "I thought Mom had a job. She's been laid off so many times this last year." She would let Homer think it was the difficulty of the decade, not because Mom was likely found unsuitable for the job. "But she's been laid off again. And now she wants my money." She shrugged. "That's all." Only it wasn't all. There was no way to recap everything in her life.

A gentle hand massaged Lena's shoulders. She turned to see that Nora had come up. She didn't say anything, but she was there. Closer than Mom had ever been when she could help it.

"Well…" There it was again—that long, drawn-out word reflecting the thoughts roaring in Homer's mind. "She is your ma. Legally, she's done got her permission to do what she will, you being so young and all."

"But she's irresponsible." Lena wished she could shrug away from Nora's comforting touch even while she yearned to bask in it. "I know her. She'll spend it all on makeup and moonshine." And who knew what else.

"Hmm." Homer clasped his hands and leaned forward. "Give me a week to study the Scriptures and see what I can find. Have you talked with Preacher?"

Lena dipped her head. She whispered, "No," but it came out so soft she doubted Homer could hear it. She couldn't talk with Pastor Stuart. Here, Homer didn't know anyone else at Willow Hollow. He didn't even know Mom. She was just a faceless name to him. It was easy to talk with him when he was so disconnected. But Pastor… she knew he suspected something, and she didn't want to be the one to solidify any thoughts that he hid behind his friendly countenance.

"The way I see it," Homer leaned back in his chair. As if that was a signal, Nora gave one final pat and shuffled back to her chair. "The head of the woman is the man. And if there ain't a man, then God gives spiritual authority to a pastor. God gives you folks to go to for counsel, Honey. But sometimes you've gotta be willing to swallow your pride and talk with them."

That wasn't what he was supposed to say. He was supposed to tell Lena that Mom was wrong—that the money could never rightfully be hers. That Lena should take the first paycheck and hightail it out away from Mom. It wasn't pride that kept her from talking to Pastor Stuart. She was protecting Mom. She was being considerate of Pastor, who was shepherding of a whole flock. Willow Hollow had plenty of people with troubles—nearly half the town was making do in this wretched depression. Pastor Stuart didn't need her complaints added to his table.

Homer picked up *The Black Arrow* and held it out to Lena. "I can see you're thinking, and I ain't gonna interrupt those thoughts no more."

She took the book. It would be so easy to crawl back into a hollow somewhere and live through Dick's miseries rather than her own.

"I reckon there'll be folks wondering what happened to their book lady today." The skin around Homer's eyes crinkled as he smiled. "Keep working, Honey. God'll give you the answers you need."

"Thank you." It was the polite thing to say. That, and a smile. Lena clutched *The Black Arrow* under her arm as Homer walked her to Kirby. She wasn't so sure God was willing to give her an answer. After all, He could have prevented Mom from her unwanted pregnancy. Or could have allowed Lena to keep this job a secret longer. Pastor Stuart said God's ways were higher than hers. It surely must be, because today, she didn't understand anything that was going on.

15

$\mathcal{L}$ena clenched the saddle horn. Here on the trail, she should be able to leave behind everything at home. Instead, it followed her. Hounded her. She closed her eyes as Kirby crossed Franklin Creek. Water splashed and she imagined her thoughts going there with the water—fleeing away, a droplet becoming nothing in the mix of the water. She smiled, hoping it would generate a better feeling within her. She had finished her route on Wednesday, like Homer had said. There were a few more readers. It was a slow growth, but Mr. Armstrong seemed to approve. She had come home to an empty house, and Mom still hadn't returned.

But today was a new day. The Lord's mercies were new for today. She had to push back the things of the past and move forward. That included worrying about today's route after three weeks of not having a single soul express interest or pay her heed, really.

There were two more bends in the trail and then she'd see the first cluster of huts. Homer had encouraged her several times that it took a while for mountain folk to warm up to new ideas—years, even. But she didn't have years. If someone else came to the library looking for work who was more competent than her, Mr. Armstrong would feel awful, but he'd do what was best for the library.

Here, the path grew too rocky for her to trust Kirby to keep sure footing. She dismounted and led Kirby—and almost jumped when she rounded the bend to find a boy seated on a rock. He looked up from his whittling. Was he sent here to warn her off before she came again?

Lena gave a hesitant smile. "Good morning."

"Ur ye the book lady?" A thick Scottish accent hung on every word.

The smile faded from Lena's lips. "I am." The boy was eleven or twelve. Old enough to be man of the house in one of the homes she'd been trying to visit—old enough to tell her to leave them alone, if he wanted to.

But he stuck out his hand. "Aidan McGrew."

"Nice to meet you, Aidan." Lena returned the handshake, her heart beginning to hope again. If he was being congenial, it wasn't likely that he was here to tell her off. "Do you— would you like to look through the books?"

"Aye!"

Lena hurried to the side and detached the saddlebags before he could change his mind—or someone would tell him not to do it.

"They telt me a *Sassenach* came on oor land."

Lena didn't know if that was positive or not. "A… what?"

Aidan grinned. "*Sassenach*. English. Low-lander."

"Is that… a problem?"

"Naw. They just dinnae take to strangers digging aroond 'ere." He took one of the books and studied its cover. "Ur all the books in English?"

"Yes…" The way the words lilted off Aidan's tongue made Lena wonder. "Can you read it?"

"Aye. I ken how to read English. My *faither* is English. But the others in the clan don't ken much English."

Things suddenly made sense to Lena. This was why they were hesitant about returning her greeting. Why none of the children responded to her questions. "So they don't just hate me?"

Aidan chuckled. "I wouldn't say that. You're a *Sassenach* for one. Stranger for two." He held up three fingers. "And, what good ur books if ye can't read them?" He slid three more books out. "Now this. They'll like this."

They were picture books. Children's books.

"Really? I'm sure I can bring more next week." She'd do anything to gain more readers and keep this route going. And with the donations they were now regularly receiving, she could customize this route.

Aidan's fingers stopped over a copy of *The Call of the Wild*.

"Would you like to borrow that one? Buck is such an amazing dog." Lena lowered her voice. "He was so torn between Thornton and the wolves. I felt so bad for him. It kept me awake until I could finish it."

Aidan flipped to the first page and Lena let him look over the words, hoping he could read well enough to get hooked.

"I'll be back next week and you can return the book. Maybe you can even read it to some of the others who can't read."

Aidan turned the page and Lena bit back a grin.

"Is that a 'yes?'"

Aidan tore his focus from the book and gave Lena a sheepish grin. "I've got meself a bonny fair hound dog. I always wondered what imaginings gaed on in their minds."

"Well, Jack London sure gave it his best effort."

Aidan closed the book and helped Lena repack the books. His eagerness over the volume was replaced by a cautionary look. "I come from the hoose on the very top." He pointed through the thick of the trees—more a directional gesture than specific. "It's nigh time fur me to help duin' the garden patch today. But I wanted to come fur I knew ye wouldn't come the length o' I lived."

"I'm glad you did, Aidan." This time, it wasn't hard to give him a smile. Even though Lena was concerned with the depths that seemed hidden behind his greenish-brown eyes.

"Give them another week. I'll read to them this week 'n' they'll fall in love wi' the books. Next week, come back 'n' I ken you'll hae a good dozen lads 'n' lasses as eager to get a book as me. They just don't ken yet."

Lena rested her hand against Kirby's saddle. "You think so?"

"I ken it."

She studied Aidan's serious expression for several seconds. She didn't have much of a reason to trust him. But... he seemed to love books as much as she did. She'd not know until she tried. "Here, take more than just one book. Some picture books?" She dug in the saddle packs for a *Peter Rabbit* and *Our Animal Friends.* "You can read them aloud. Maybe teach them how to read some of the words themselves."

Aidan looked at the books for a moment before reaching out to take them. "I'll take good care o' them. I promise."

"I know you will."

Lena watched as Aidan scampered back up the path. That wasn't the answer to her prayers that she had expected, but she wasn't going to complain. She could return to Mr. Armstrong with a positive report on Friday, for once.

A song bubbled in her heart as she led Kirby a few steps down the trail before mounting. The ride back to Willow Hollow took much less time than it had coming to the mountains in the predawn. She'd see if Mr. Armstrong needed help organizing new book donations. She'd ask him about children's picture books and maybe books to help young readers.

She stopped by the stables first.

"Is something wrong?" Jed took Kirby's reins and glanced over him.

"Everything is just fine." Lena gave a cheery smile as she dismounted. "I met this boy, Aidan, who said he'd actually help get the people interested in books. I didn't have to do my route because he said wait until next time and they'll be chomping at the bits to come get books after he's read to some of them." She took a deep breath and felt her cheeks go warm as she realized how much she had just rambled.

Jed gave a friendly smile as he detached the saddlebags. "That's great. I'll bring these back to the library while you unsaddle."

This time, she didn't argue about his help. "Thanks, Jed."

She almost felt like whistling as she put the tack back on the hooks and brushed Kirby down. Jed returned and took Kirby to get some feed. Lena kept herself from skipping to the Building and wove her way to the library. Books that hadn't yet been organized stacked up beside Mr. Armstrong's desk.

He looked up and concern flashed over his face until his eyes met Lena's. Confusion replaced the concern.

Lena tried to keep her voice low as she filled him in on the details. He grinned. "That's wonderful news." The excited undertones lacing his words gave Lena a glimmer of hope. She was doing all right on the job so far. She wanted to believe it.

"Yes sir, she's here all right. Just walked in the library."

Someone's loud voice bellowed from the center room of the Building.

A man appeared at the doorway of the library. "Miss Davis?" The man's suit was a dark gray with windowpane pattern. An olive green tie was tucked underneath the buttoned coat.

Lena's thoughts instantly went to Mom and her throat went dry. This was a city man, too fine for the likes of Willow Hollow.

"Is there somewhere private we can talk?"

Lena looked at Mr. Armstrong, her eyes wide. He stepped away from his desk and patted her on the shoulder. "I'll step out, and the library is all yours."

She didn't exactly want Mr. Armstrong to leave her alone with this stranger—but then, if it had anything to do with Mom, she for sure didn't want him to stay. The door closed, and Lena was left alone. She curled her toes in her shoes and looked down at the faded wooden floor. It needed a new coat of stain. She hadn't noticed it before.

"Miss Davis." The man's voice was low-toned. Cultured. Smooth.

She tilted her head up a little, looking at the man's chin. He was smooth-shaven with a strong scent of spiced citrus.

"I'm Mr. Jeffreys. I've tried to locate your mother. Do you know where she is?"

Lena raised her eyebrows. This was what he needed a private audience for? "No sir, she hasn't been home for a few days." She cringed as her tone matched the cultured intonation of Mr. Jeffreys.

His lips thinned and he nodded. "I was afraid of such. I dislike burdening a child such as yourself…"

She bristled. What had Mom done this time? A man from the city had never taken the bother to come out to Willow Hollow before on Mom's behalf, as far as Lena knew.

Mr. Jeffreys pulled out a thin envelope from the depths of his coat pocket. "I have sent your mother six notices and she hasn't replied." He held the envelope out to her. "See that she gets this. And tell her I have been gracious in waiting, but this time I cannot wait longer."

Lena's throat went dry as Mr. Jeffreys' pushed the envelope into her hands. "Wait… for what?"

"The letter explains. Good day, Miss Davis."

He left the library and Lena looked down at the crisp envelope in her hands. She had no idea when Mom would be home, and Mr. Jeffreys' business seemed urgent. What kind of threat did this letter pose? She looked around the library then slowly slit open the envelope. Bold letters across the top of the page read,

Notice of eviction.

16

$\mathcal{I}$t was past midnight, but Lena was still wide awake.

What had happened? They owned this house. Mom's parents had bought it for her. Someone couldn't evict them from a place they owned. She refused to think that Mom had gotten a mortgage and hidden the fact behind lies. They didn't need it. Sure, things were a little tight now and then, but Mom more or less kept a job. They didn't have electricity bills to pay like in the city. All they had to do was pay a few insurance notes. There was no need to mortgage it.

The outside steps creaked, and the screen door flipped open. Lena sat up in bed as Mom walked in, not attempting to be quiet at this late hour. She started toward her room, bulging bags on each arm, without even a glance at Lena.

"Mom!" The word came out in a hiss from all the pent-up questions and worries Lena had roiled in her mind since yesterday afternoon.

Mom stopped. Her shoulders relaxed, and she released an exasperated sigh. Likely her eyes were rolled upward.

"Why aren't you sleeping yet? Don't you have church tomorrow?"

"Were you going to let our house be sold out from under us?" Lena bit her lip to keep it from quivering.

Mom's shoulders snapped straight, and she spun around. Her words came out even and measured, "What are you talking about?"

"The mortgage. A Mr. Jeffreys…"

"He had no business talking with you."

Lena swallowed. She wasn't going to tell Mom she snooped in her mail. "Are… are you going to use my money to pay him? Or…" The bags or merchandise seemed to taunt Lena. "Were you going to use it for your frivolous shopping? How much did you pay for what's in those bags? Enough for a month's rent? And he said you haven't paid him in over six months." Lena stopped abruptly when Mom laid her burdens on the floor. It must have been the fear making her so bold. "I—I didn't mean…"

"Oh yes, you did mean it." Mom took a step forward. "Just like every other time you've sassed me. Don't think you're a perfect child, just because you go to church. You'll never be like the others there. Go on pretending as long as you wish. I'm sick of it all."

Lena pulled the tattered quilt up to her chin and curled against the wall, trying to block out as many of Mom's words as she could. "When were you going to tell me?" Her voice came out small and weak.

"I'm not going to be evicted." In the dim light, Lena saw Mom punch the air. Her voice was like flint crashing against flint—hard, unyielding, sparking. "I can fix this. Your money will see to that."

116

There were so many questions Lena wished she had asked Mr. Jeffreys. But the shock of the letter had made any logical thought process flee from her mind and she had no strength to chase him down for answers. "But… I only make twenty-eight dollars a month. We've got months of payments to make up for. And the letter says we have until the end of the month. I don't get my first paycheck until the end of the month."

"Twenty-eight dollars will do." Mom's voice was smooth and blasé.

"I don't think he'll listen."

"Oh, but he will. Just leave it to me."

The way Mom said it made Lena's insides quiver.

"And if not, I can find somewhere in the city." Mom turned on her heel.

But there was one more question Lena had. "When did you mortgage the house?"

Mom's perfect curls bobbed as she tilted her head. "Oh, too far back for me to remember." Her tone was light as she picked up her bags and entered her room. "I needed the money." The door closed firmly, and the lock slid in place.

I… Always "I" with Mom. Never "we." Lena pulled the quilt over her head and squeezed her eyes shut. She wouldn't let the tears come. There was a return address on the envelope. Something fancy sounding. She'd write Mr. Jeffreys. Beg him to reconsider. Explain to him Mom's irrational behavior and spending habits. Something. Anything to keep them from the streets. Or—she swallowed as the first tear escaped down her cheek—to keep herself from the streets. Mom would see that *she* wouldn't go homeless, regardless of what happened to Lena. Mom probably already had plans to escape to the city like she'd long wanted to do.

The next morning in church, Lena kept her head down and entered late. She could feel Mr. Armstrong's curious and sympathetic gaze as he whispered a "good morning" when she passed his pew. She ignored him and slid into an empty seat—not quite as close to the wall as she preferred, but far enough back to where she could still slip away without being noticed.

"This morning, my thoughts come from Psalm 37." Pastor Stuart's voice was confident as he stood to preach. "It's one of those Psalms that I love turning to whenever my soul feels in need of that extra special reminder of God's comfort, guidance, and grace. Let's read a few verses now, beginning with verse three."

Lena flipped to the Psalm and read along. She needed that comfort, guidance, and grace now more than ever.

"Trust in the LORD, and do good; so shalt thou dwell in the land, and verily thou shalt be fed."

Well, that was a beautiful promise. But the hope Lena was clinging to was quickly shredding as Mom's choices sliced through her every effort.

"Delight thyself also in the LORD; and he shall give thee the desires of thine heart."

Hadn't she tried? She didn't want much. Just a little security in her life—but now it was all being taken away from her.

"Commit thy way unto the LORD; trust also in him; and he shall bring it to pass. And he shall bring forth righteousness as the light, and thy judgment as the noonday."

How was God going to bring her way to pass if Mom was constantly working against her? Against God Himself?

"Rest in the LORD, and wait patiently for him: fret not thyself because of him who prospereth in his way, because of the man who bringeth wicked devices to pass."

There wasn't time to rest. It was time to *do* something to get out of this mess Mom had created.

"Cease from anger, and forsake wrath: fret not thyself in any wise to do evil."

She wasn't fretting to do evil—it was Mom who was bent on it. The bitter thought that Mom should be here, listening to these verses, threaded its way through Lena's mind. She wasn't going to get angry over it. She'd find a solution.

As Pastor Stuart worked his way through the points, Lena tried to listen while working out a solution.

"Give Him our worries. The Lord can take care of every single problem we have—He is fully capable; we won't be able to figure things out by worrying over them. 1 Peter 5:7 says, 'Casting all your care upon Him; for He careth for you.'"

I can ask Mr. Clark for another extension. He'll be more pliable than that Mr. Jeffreys.

"Give Him our will. Our wants, our desires. When we delight in the Lord, He changes our desires and gives us *those* desires."

Maybe Mr. Clark will even have a job that I can take on. Or I can ask Pastor Stuart if he has need of help in the stables. Probably not, since Jed worked there and had more experience than Lena, though he was younger.

"Give Him our path. There are a lot of ways our flesh says is right but the Bible says is wrong—the way the Bible leads us is *always* for our good. God already knows the route because He created the map."

I can ask Homer if he'll even let me stay with him and Nora, if Mr. Jeffreys does boot us out.

"Give Him our weariness. We find rest when we trust, delight, and commit."

Pastor Stuart stepped out from behind the pulpit, signaling the close of the service. "Matthew 11:28 promises, 'Come unto me, all ye that labor and are heavy laden, and I will give you rest.' He holds nothing back. Will you?"

Lena stood with the rest of the congregation and closed her eyes when invitation was given. *Lord, I need Your help. Please show me what I am to do. And change Mom. Please, please, Lord... change Mom.*

She was too far in to slip out unnoticed, so she waited her turn to shake Pastor Stuart's hand and pretend everything was fine in her world. *Hypocrite.* That's all Mom thought she was. And maybe she was. But she genuinely loved Jesus Christ and came to church because she needed this reprieve from normal life—not just from a sense of duty. She wasn't fully hypocritical, even if she did blink away the frown that wanted to surface and presented Pastor Stuart with a smile she hoped was free from pain.

She exchanged the expected pleasantries with the pastor and turned to walk home.

"Miss Book Lady!"

Lena froze, almost expecting the call to have been made for one of the other librarians on route. But no, it was Jack

Odis who came running toward her. His face was red from the dash down the mountain.

Lena left the crowd and joined him. "What are you doing down here?"

Jack paused to suck in air. "Aunt Nora… Uncle…"

"Did something happen?" Panic streaked through Lena like a bolt of lightning.

"She's… bad off…" His breathing still hadn't regulated. "Uncle wants a doctor… preacher… too…"

There could only be one reason Homer would want a preacher and the doctor. Lena's stomach flipped as she spun to find Dr. Casey, who stood several inches above the average person.

"Please…" Jack grabbed Lena's arm, his eyes wide in fright. "Hurry…"

17

$\mathcal{T}$ears coursed down Lena's cheeks as she watched dirt clods land on the crude wooden coffin that now held Nora's frail body. Doctor Casey had said it was too late—that the dementia had taken its course and it was Nora's time to go. Pastor Stuart had been there to offer a prayer at the time of Nora's passing. Was here now, saying gentle words as Homer laid his bride to rest.

The children's faces were all serious. The younger ones crying because their mothers were crying, the older boys frowning and refusing to shed a tear, the girls joining the adults with their vocal mourning.

The hours passed in a blur. Pastor Stuart left, then one by one, the various families left, promising to look after Homer that evening. Lena's legs grew weak, and she sank onto a log several feet away from the fresh grave. It wasn't like Willow Hollow's graveyard here. The weather-beaten stones with crude names and dates carved on them weren't aligned at perfect angles, but they still all faced the east.

She hadn't been to a funeral since Aunt Melba Lynn's passing, and that was so long ago. Memories of Nora's feeble hand pressing her shoulder when Nora couldn't understand the turmoil going on in Lena's mind surfaced with renewed vigor. Lena should have expressed her gratitude. She should have reached out to the woman more. Stayed and read her some stories to give Homer a break.

Homer stayed with his head bowed, his hands limp by his sides. When the sun lowered, casting deep shadows across the land, he turned and walked to Lena. Without a word, he sank onto the log beside her.

"I love her. My precious bride." His voice came out strong and with a hint of a smile.

Lena folded her hands over her knees and waited.

"She was the purdiest thing I ever set eyes on. Smart too. She could read circles around me. Could tell when was the best plantin' time. She took care of everything while I was away at war. Never once did her letters make me feel like I was needed home. She could take care of it all, my Nora." He leaned forward and placed his elbows on his knees. "You didn't know her at her best. She's been gone for a few years now—her mind, that is. It still pains something to lose her in the flesh, though. I could look at her and see…" His voice cracked and he paused. "I could see who she always was, not the woman she had become. Oh, she had a temper all right." He chuckled. "Was competitive. But she'd give anything to anyone who came needin' it. A more gracious soul you'd never seen."

The silence hung between them for several long minutes. What must it be like, to lose someone so dear to you? Lena wasn't as strong as Homer. She'd be back home in misery. What she saw here couldn't be described in a book. That fresh, raw grief—yet quiet, gentle hope and peace.

"These last years have been hard years," Homer said. "She kept waking, saying something was out there. Couldn't remember how to do nothin'. But I vowed to take her till death parted us, and I aimed before God to keep that promise. I also vowed 'for better and for worse.' Lately, it seems as if there was more 'worse' than 'better,' but I wouldn't go changin' these days for nothing. She's made me a better man—even when her mind wasn't there. That in and of itself has made me better. More patient. More gentle. Loving. Oh, I've had to pray a lot. I didn't feel like loving her every day. Not when she didn't give me much sleep then demanded my attention." Homer gave a small, sad smile. "But even in the challenges, God helped me to learn. To grow. I'm not too old to be learnin', I figured. I wouldn't change it for nothin'. All these years, she'd done served me, fixed me food, woke early to cook me a big, hot breakfast every mornin'. Never once complained, my bride."

Homer looked off in the distance. "It's coming nigh on dusk." He stood a bit slower than usual then held out a hand to Lena. "Don't want you out too late. Best get you on home."

Home. She hadn't thought of that place much these last few days. She wanted more than anything to unburden her heart and troubles to Homer, but now wasn't the time. And it wouldn't be the time before their deadline was up. She tamped down the fears that arose and turned to Homer. He still held onto her hand, much like she'd always imagine her daddy would have, had he cared to stick around. She reached up and wrapped her arms around Homer. He patted her on the shoulder.

"Thanks for bein' here, Honey. Means the world to this old man."

Without another word, Homer released her and turned back to the grave. She sensed without any words that it was his time to say a final, silent farewell to his beloved bride. Lena walked through the tombstones—some tall and long, others short and squat—until she reached Kirby, ready and waiting for her as always. It would be dark by the time she reached Willow Hollow, but surely even Widow Burman couldn't think ill of her.

Homer's words echoed through her mind as she descended the mountain. Oh, to be loved as Homer loved Nora. But all Lena had was a harsh, selfish mom whose lifestyle would frighten any upright young man from seriously pursuing her. But it was more than that. It was Homer's whole attitude. Lena had seen how frail and weak Nora was. She hadn't known all the details of her keeping Homer awake—yet Homer had never looked at Nora with bitterness, just love. Compassion. Patience. Yet he said it was Nora's challenges that had made him this man that Lena knew. He saw the challenges as something from which to learn.

Lena gripped the saddle horn and leaned back slightly to balance herself with Kirby's steps.

Homer had accused Lena of using a book to hide from life's challenges. Not in so many words, but the implications had been clear. And she knew what he indicated was true.

She saw challenges as something to avoid at all cost. It was too painful to live through them and glean some spiritual lesson. Too hard.

Give Him our weariness.

She could hear Pastor Stuart's voice clearly. It wasn't something that had been said at the funeral but at church, Sunday. Lena focused her mind, recalling the other main points.

Give Him our worries. Give Him our will. Give Him our path.

How was she to do that when Mom was working against anything she wanted to do? Finally, when it seemed like Lena could take a step forward, Mom's actions were a mudslide, burying any hopes Lena had in a sludge of sin, debt, and self-absorption.

Pastor Stuart's offer to help if she needed it surfaced before her mind. It was too late tonight to tramp to his house and demand an hour of his time. Today had been her day off. Tomorrow she had a route. And then Thursday was the twenty-seventh. Two days before the deadline. Too late, in so many ways.

And it was her fault.

She pulled in the reins and Kirby stopped. He had to be hungry for something other than mere nibbles of mountain grass, but he was patient and followed her commands. Once, Pastor Stuart had likened following God like a horse following its master. A good horse wouldn't question its rider's commands but heed immediately.

"But Lord, what do you want me to do?" Lena wanted to scream the words into the night air, but her lips could only form the words silently.

18

$\mathcal{T}$he minutes of the day seemed to speed by without stopping. Even though Lena pushed Kirby to go faster on the route, she was slowed by a rush of children who wanted new books. She should be grateful—would have been grateful last week. But that was before everything in life threatened to dislodge. She had wanted to get back to Willow Hollow before dark, but the sun had sunk behind the mountains a good thirty minutes before. So much for her hopes of talking with Pastor Stuart. It was too late—again.

She'd prayed all day and so far, God was silent. Or maybe she just didn't know how to listen for Him. But there was nothing—no ideas, no solutions, no direction.

Now, she let Kirby have his head. He didn't have to be pushed to trot through town to the stables awaiting him with the promise of a handful of oats and release from the saddle. Lena mechanically lit the lantern, put the saddle where it belonged, and scooped out some oats. As Kirby munched them, she brushed him down, taking more time than was required for this task.

Mom hadn't been home last night, but that didn't mean she'd be away tonight. It was likely, but Lena wasn't ready to go to their little shack and find out.

She wove her fingers around Kirby's black mane. Realization hit her. When they lost the house, she'd most likely lose her job, which meant she had only one more day with Kirby. A sob welled inside her heart and tore through her. She buried her face in Kirby's neck as another sob followed.

"Lena?"

Lena's heart dropped. She'd been caught, even if it was only Jed. She tried to silence her sobs, but it only made them worse.

"Is everything all right?"

She hugged Kirby tighter, wishing her grip on him would help her get a grip on her tears.

"Are you hurt?"

Just go away, Jed. She didn't need him. She didn't need anyone to see her blubber like this. Mom would be mortified.

"Let me get Da."

Lena fought against the sobs as she heard Jed run away. By the time he returned, she had stopped the main sobs, but tears were still streaming down her cheeks.

"Aw, Honey." It was Mrs. Stuart—not Pastor—who spoke and enveloped Lena in a hug. "Go on home, Jed, be sure the girls are in bed."

For once, Lena felt protected and secure. The sobs came all over again. Lena couldn't remember a time when Mom had hugged her. Aunt Melba Lynn had, once, when Lena broke her arm and was terrified when the doctor wanted to touch it. But that was more to control Lena than comfort her.

"Shh…" Mrs. Stuart rocked her gently.

Lena didn't know how long it was before she gained control and wiped her tears clean. She drew back from Mrs. Stuart.

"What's wrong, child?" Mrs. Stuart brushed the hair from Lena's forehead.

Lena glanced around and realized Pastor Stuart had come after all, patiently waiting on a milk stool across from them.

She swallowed as she collapsed onto an extra stool, not sure how to begin. Pastor and Mrs. Stuart waited. She shut her eyes and thought back. They would have to know everything—her history, Mom's harsh words, Mom's monetary indiscretions, her tendency to the Higgins' moonshine… but also Lena sneaking the job behind Mom's back. She was a failure. A disappointment to the church. And they didn't even know it. She took a deep breath and opened her eyes. "A-are you sure? It may take a while."

Pastor reached over and pulled out another stool for Mrs. Stuart then said, "Honey, we've got time for you. Go ahead."

The care in their eyes made Lena's heart bleed. She started at the beginning—with Mom's true history, with her true history, or as far as she knew it. Spending days with Aunt Melba Lynn while Mom was away in the big city, then alone after Aunt Melba Lynn passed on. How she survived her few years of school alone, without any true friends. All the way up to this past month with Mr. Jeffreys. The thought of losing her home was now a dull throb thrumming in time with her heartbeat. Her tears were completely dry by now. She wasn't sure she even cared about life anymore. It had done nothing pleasant to her—well, besides offering her books with the fantasy of an agreeable life. But that's all it was. A fantasy. In real life there was pain, sorrow, and hurt. So much hurt.

There was silence when she finished. She didn't want to look at Pastor or his wife. She didn't want to see the judgment in their eyes. The criticism for her hiding behind the truth all these years. For pretending she was just another upright Christian, when sin and deceit shaded her very existence.

"I didn't know." Pastor's voice was soft and gentle, tinted with regret. That couldn't be, though. None of this was his fault. "I tried reaching out to your mom, but not much to you. I'm sorry, Lena. We could have helped more over the years."

Lena dared to glance at his blue eyes. They still held that genuine care—not judgment.

She shrugged her shoulder. "But… what can I do… *now*…?" Now that she was on the verge of losing her home, her mom, and her job.

Pastor Stuart leaned back. "I don't know. But you're not going to face this alone, Lena. It's what God has put the church together for—to bear one another's burdens when they're too hard to bear. And you, my dear, have such a burden."

"But… you can't let Mom know." Lena's heart thudded at the thought. If Mom thought for one minute that she had blabbed to Pastor Stuart in order to get the freedom she wanted or to smudge dirt on Mom's already questionable character… she wouldn't understand the pressure forcing words to spill from Lena's heart.

"I can't promise that. She's your mother—your God-given authority. I can't do anything behind her back."

Lena wrapped her feet around two of the milk stool's legs. Her hands fisted on her lap and her throat tightened.

"But," Pastor Stuart continued, "We'll do everything to make sure she won't harm you more."

"She's going to blame me. Or…" Lena lifted one of her shoulders. She didn't even know what Mom would do. It all depended on how sober Mom was. She rubbed her arm subconsciously, already feeling how Mom's fingers would dig into them. *Do I have to go home tonight?*

"No, Honey. We can find you a place in our home for tonight at least. I know Lillian would welcome you into her room."

Lena looked at Mrs. Stuart wide-eyed. "I—I didn't mean to speak aloud…" Heat radiated from her face.

Pastor Stuart stood and held out a hand to Mrs. Stuart then Lena. When they were all three standing, he bowed his head and began praying. Lena didn't hear any of it. Her eyes blurred with tears. She knew how crowded the Stuart home was, especially now that Lillian was staying there. It wasn't a solution. Not anymore than it would be to track down Mr. Jeffreys and pretend she had the payment in full. She finally closed her eyes and bowed her head.

God, I didn't get myself into this mess—and I'm doubting right now that You can help me out of it.

"Help us to fully trust in Your will and hope in Your goodness…"

Lena sucked in a deep breath. She didn't think she had a strand of hope left. Maybe Pastor Stuart had enough. But she doubted it.

19

*L*ena slowly eased herself to a sitting position. She had tried to convince Mrs. Stuart to put her on the floor, but instead, Lillian had given her the bed and had created a pallet on the floor for herself. It wouldn't have mattered where Lena lay down—she couldn't get much sleep.

She tiptoed to the front door and pulled on her coat then slipped outside, leaving Lillian asleep. It was about the same time she usually headed to the library when on route—before dawn, before Lillian, Mr. Armstrong, Edna Sue, or anyone else from the library was there; before Willow Hollow was awake. She hurried to the stables and worked quickly to ready Kirby. Today was the last day. Tomorrow she'd have to have a solution and still, God seemed silent. Even after Pastor Stuart had prayed.

She mounted and led Kirby out of Willow Hollow. The town was still asleep, no one to care if she was setting off on her last grand adventure. She placed her hands tensely on the saddle horn. She was clinging tightly already, as if Kirby was picking his way up steep inclines.

She glanced around and her eyes caught a glimpse of a curtain dropping down and Widow Burman's words from that day in the store burned in her mind. *He's watching you, girl, you know that, right?*

Not everyone in Willow Hollow was Widow Burman. Lena had repeated the barn incident with Pastor and Mrs. Stuart over and over in her mind. They didn't have a solution, but somehow, just knowing that they knew gave Lena a sense of peace she'd never experienced before. She stared at the Widow's curtained window as she passed. While there were many out there who wouldn't believe her motives and actions, there were so many more who were willing to reach out a hand to help and love her, if she only opened up to let them.

Was that how God was? Just waiting for her to reach out more to Him instead of expecting her to solve all her problems herself?

The thought kept Lena occupied as Kirby climbed up the mountainside. The sun rose and spread its warmth across the mountain. Lena stopped in front of Homer's cabin. The door swung open. Homer smiled as he came out.

"I thought that sounded like ol' Kirby's hooves." He held out a napkin. "I thought you might just come on your day off. I 'preciate it, Honey."

Lena dismounted, hiding her face as it had to be pulsing red. She wished she could say she came just to keep Homer company, but she knew it was more than that. She was reaching out again—this time, it was easier than when she had tried with Pastor Stuart. Homer knew her better. Had heard her story before last night.

"Come on." Homer waved for Lena to follow. They settled on a rock just a few feet from the front door. It gave Lena a clear view of a ravine.

She fingered the biscuit, pressing a few crumbs together then slipping them in her mouth. "We're losing our home." The harsh, unvarnished, blunt truth. She had no desire to make it even sound better. "What did I do wrong?" Lena swallowed as sobs suddenly threatened to surface. If she started again, she wasn't sure she would stop. "I've tried. I've tried to do everything that Mom wanted. I've tried to be the daughter I should. Nothing is good enough. She always looks at me the same way. She always acts the same way— as if I'm not a part of her life." She pinched another section off the biscuit and rolled it into a small ball.

Homer cleared his throat. "Sometimes, it ain't you. Relationships are more than twofold. They're threefold: you and God, her and God, and you and her." He paused and rubbed his face. "You can only deal with the two you're a part of: you and God, you and her. Ya gotta let her deal with the relationship between her and God—and until she gets that straight, it'll be hard for her to have a good relationship with you, even if you're trying."

"But I want to have a good relationship with her." Now that she said the words, she realized the truth. She wanted a mom she could talk to, a mom who would care for her and cheer her on. "How can I do that when she refuses to change?" Mom hadn't changed, all these years. And she wouldn't.

Lena set the biscuit aside and leaned forward, resting her arms on her knees and gripping her hands together.

"Honey, you can't force someone to have a good relationship with you. You can only keep loving them as Christ loves you, keep forgiving them as Christ forgives you, and keep reaching out to them as Christ does to you."

Homer reached over and placed one of his old, calloused hands over Lena's. "Do what you can do, and leave the results up to Jesus Christ and His timing. He alone can soften a heart and direct it toward Him. He alone can mend her broken heart and heal her—you can't. All you can do is pray and hope."

But how long would it take? They had only until tomorrow night… and then what?

"Ya know that verse in Galatians?" Homer leaned back. It wasn't until then Lena noticed he had brought along the Bible she had supplied him. "That one about sowing and reaping… here… 'Be not deceived; God is not mocked: for whatsoever a man soweth, that shall he also reap.' That sowing and reaping can be fleshly and spiritually. Your mom—she's done a lot of sowing in her life. It's come time she has to do some reaping—facing the penalty of the choices she's made. But that don't just affect her. It affects you too. Remember this, Lena: whatever you sow is gonna be reaped in more than your life alone. Others'll have some reaping to do."

Lena swallowed. Her very existence was a product of Mom's sowing. And Mom hadn't liked the reaping that much. A tear swept down her cheek. Mom couldn't blame her—not for being here, not for changing Mom's life. The realization jarred her.

"You've gotta look at your life, though. Sow unforgiveness and you'll reap deeply-rooted bitterness that takes years to weed out." Homer flipped through his Bible, the sound of rustling pages soothing Lena. "'Let all bitterness… be put away from you… And be ye kind one to another, tenderhearted, forgiving one another, even as God for Christ's sake hath forgiven you.' That's in Ephesians chapter four. Bitterness is an invisible weed that creeps in when we're not trying to be kind, tenderhearted, and forgiving. It sneaks in when we forget all Christ has done for *us* and refuse to show that grace to others."

Homer turned toward Lena, his blue eyes full of care. "I know you're worried about where to live, Lena. I know you want to keep your job, but those are temporal things. God has promised not to let His seed go begging bread. He's gonna take care of you. You need to think about the deeper issues that are threatening here. You need to think about the sowing you're doing today that you and others will have to reap on tomorrow." He flipped through more pages, though it wasn't as if he was looking for something—just moving. "I know I'm preaching at you, but if this old man can teach you one thing, it's to avoid the path he's been on before. Learn from those who have gone before you. You don't have to walk that path, too."

He closed his Bible and gently patted Lena's knee. "I'm praying for you—for you and your mother. But think about these things." He slowly stood up and walked back to his house, leaving Lena alone.

For years she had seen herself as the one who caused difficulty in their family. And for years, she had tried to live a life completely opposite to Mom's—no unnecessary spending, no laziness, no big city, no men, no moonshine.

She had been so scared of becoming her mom in all these areas that she didn't realize she was Mom all over again in her attitude and actions. Blaming others. Harboring bitterness. Looking at others' lives when she should have been focusing on herself and her walk with God.

She stood up and smoothed out her skirt before mounting Kirby again. There were a lot of things she had to think over on the ride home.

20

*L*ena pulled on the reins. Just two more bends, and she'd see Willow Hollow. Things were still as unclear for the future as they had been last night, but after talking with the Stuarts and Homer, a load had shifted. She wasn't bearing this burden alone. In addition to God's care for her, there were people—real flesh and blood—who loved her and were reaching out to help her. Tears stung her eyes, but they felt different than the ones she had cried last night on Mrs. Stuart's shoulder.

She stopped Kirby before they reached Willow Hollow. He stopped easily and let her dismount before dipping his head to snatch a bite from early growth. Lena flipped his reins around a tree, secure enough to where he wouldn't free himself, then wandered off the path. She wasn't going anywhere in particular. She just wasn't ready to face Willow Hollow. Not yet. Not while her mind was still whirling with everything. She brushed dried pine needles from a boulder and sank onto it. A few birds twittered in the late-morning air. Breeze whispered through the trees, toying with Lena's frayed jacket but not piercing through with winter's ice.

Lena's eyes slid shut.

You're worthless. It's your fault. You'll never amount to anything. Useless. Careless girl. Your fault. Your fault. Your fault.

The words hammered through her mind in Mom's shrill voice. Then they changed to Lena's own voice. *My fault. Worthless, reckless sinner.*

Then it was Pastor Stuart's voice interrupting. *The Lord can take care of every single problem we have—He is fully capable; we won't be able to figure things out by worrying over them.*

Even problems she had carried for almost sixteen years of life?

Casting all your care upon Him, for He careth for you.

All. That meant all. Everything. Holding nothing back.

"Lord, I don't know what to do. I'm trying to cast my cares on You, but they're too heavy. I need to know what the next step is."

You've got to look at your life. Sow unforgiveness and you'll reap deeply-rooted bitterness that takes years to weed out.

Homer had pointed out the eternal, while she had been focusing only on the temporal. She rested her elbows on her knees and laid her head in her hands, her fingers weaving through her loose hair.

Images of Mom flashed before her: Mom coming in with a new dress, spending hours styling her hair, her brows furrowed at Lena's presence, her harsh words, her eyes bleary with the effects of moonshine. Each time a new image appeared, Lena cringed. Was this what bitterness was? Hanging onto these memories that weren't edifying? Clinging to the words that burned like acid in her heart? Reliving every hurt that Mom had inflicted upon her? Wishing that she could do something to finally stand up for herself? Wanting Mom to feel just a piece of the pain she had forced upon Lena all these years?

Forgive, even as God for Christ's sake hath forgiven you.

She knew she was forgiven. It was five years ago when she finally understood how much God loved her—Lena, an unwanted child of an unwed mother, banned from her rich family and mistrusted by half of the community in which she lived. But God loved her. Unconditionally. She knew what "agape" love meant. She loved the history portions in Psalms and knew how often God forgave the Israelites when they had turned their backs on Him.

This was the type of forgiveness He wanted her to extend to others. To Mom.

"God… I can't do it."

I can do all things through Christ which strengtheneth me.

Okay, maybe she could. It was just going to be a long journey. And she was ready for everything to smooth out today.

What did forgiveness look like? Lena wished she had thought to bring her Bible along. She was pretty sure she would find forgiveness as forgetting that which was behind and reaching forward to that which is before. Why was it so hard to forgive, yet so easy to remember the pains and hurts and nurture bitterness? Was forgiveness pushing aside the feelings Mom had nurtured in her and instead choosing to love? Bringing every harmful word she had heard to God and leaving it in His capable hands?

Bitterness wouldn't give her a place to live. It would just destroy any semblance of peace she had left. She knew that—she had seen it lived before her in Mom's very existence. But she had been blind to its seedlings taking root in her own heart.

Lena let out a rush of air. "Lord, I can't do this on my own. I need Your help." Every day. Every hour. Every minute. She knew how often those thoughts would come up. How often she'd have to battle the temptation to become bitter. To blame Mom for everything.

But today... today, she chose to forgive. And tomorrow she'd have to make that choice again.

She finally stood. The sun was well overhead, but Kirby was waiting patiently for her where she had left him.

"Let's get us on home, boy."

Except she didn't have a home. Or wouldn't, after tomorrow. She swallowed. Willow Hollow was her home. Somehow, she'd find a way to stay there instead of roaming the city streets with Mom.

The movements of town seemed subdued. No one paid her mind as Lena led Kirby to the stables and returned him to his stall. She straightened her shoulders and walked across the street to the Building. She didn't have to be at the library today, but there wasn't a place she'd rather be. It was a better option than going home, if Mom happened to be there. Lena walked into the Building and across the wooden planks to her safe haven. She placed her hand on the knob of the library door. It swung open and out of her grasp and she stood face-to-face with Mom.

"There you are." Mom had the good graces to sound worried in public, but her expression—visible only to Lena—was shrewd. She snapped the closure of her clutch. "I was looking for you."

"I was just… thinking…" Lena couldn't bring herself to look Mom in the eye. She didn't want to see the hatred there. The unhappiness—with *her*.

"Thinking doesn't get you anywhere, Lena. You have to get out of your daydream world and into this one. Look at me!" Mom had lowered her voice, and while her tone seemed pleasant, her lips hardened into a frown. "Mr. Jeffreys came by. It's done. We're homeless." She laid a hand on Lena's shoulder. It probably looked like a tender touch to onlookers, but Lena felt Mom's fingers tighten and dig into her flesh. "You keep working here. I'm going to the city."

Lena blinked as tears surfaced. "You're… where… what about…?" She couldn't phrase any questions.

"You found a job without my help. You can find a place to live the same way. You don't need me." The words were flippant. Almost excited. Like Mom had waited for this moment since the day Lena had been born. Mom gave Lena a pat on the shoulder. "Take care."

Mom brushed past Lena. A few seconds later, Lena heard the outside door of the Building latch shut.

The shelves of the library came into view. Lena was still standing here, in front of the door.

"Lena?"

She brushed the tears away and looked up at Mr. Armstrong as he stepped closer. "Are you feeling all right? You look terrible."

How was she supposed to answer that one? Mom's actions shouldn't surprise her. She had been half-expecting it. But her stubborn heart had clung to the hope that maybe, perhaps, Mom cared enough for her to ride this storm out with her. How naive to wish that.

"Here."

Mr. Armstrong grabbed her hand and Lena felt herself almost pushed into a chair then Mr. Armstrong's hands settled comfortably on her shoulders.

If she had a few dollars, maybe she could appease Mr. Jeffreys—talk him into one more month staying at their place. Give her time to figure something out. Even if she had to visit the dreaded big city to do it.

"When… when can I get my paycheck?"

Mr. Armstrong's hands fell from her shoulders, and Lena winced. That was blunt. She hated that she even had to ask. It sounded like she didn't trust Mr. Armstrong to hold up his end of the deal.

Mr. Armstrong blinked once. Slowly. "Your mom just left with your paycheck. She said you were sick. That is, that you wouldn't be here to collect it tomorrow. I—I'm sorry."

Lena's heart dropped to the floor. Mom didn't—she wouldn't—be so selfish and heartless. All of her resolutions from just a few minutes before fled away, replaced by raw anger. Lena ran out the Building, but the daily bus had already left, leaving her behind. Motherless and penniless.

21

*N*otice of eviction.

The unforgiving paper flapped on the door as Lena looked around the room she had spent so many hours in. The only home she had known besides her days spent at Aunt Melba Lynn's. It wasn't much in her pitiful life, but it was all she knew. Mr. Jeffreys was still there—apparently from when Mom had met with him. It was difficult, but Lena had finally gained permission to comb through the home and retrieve her belongings. They weren't much. Mom had almost swept the house clean. No food was left in the cupboard. No candles on the tables. Just the pathetic blanket that Lena slept with, the two sets of extra clothes she had, and her Bible. Lena clutched her belongings and stood as Mr. Jeffreys stepped inside, making no effort to soften the stomp of his well-polished shoes.

Lena tilted her head up just enough to acknowledge his presence without looking him in the eye. "Thank you, sir."

He gave a polished, polite dip of his head, but Lena could feel his eyes searing her with condescension.

She slipped past him and ran through the cluster of houses. She was never going to come back to this section of Willow Hollow. It was her past. Behind her. Something she would forget. Gladly. Forget, and forgive.

Lena clutched the bundle. It was all she had. No money. No food. Just some rags of clothes and a blanket. And a job. Mr. Armstrong's words had almost tripped over each other as he had rushed after her to apologize and assure her she had the job still—and that she was doing an amazing job for one so young.

Mom may have tried, but she hadn't stolen quite everything away from her.

Today, I will forgive.

It was easier to say in the mountain breeze than right after a fresh wound that tore her heart open. She took a deep breath as she neared Main Street. Mr. Armstrong and Pastor were standing on the Building's porch deep in conversation. Mr. Armstrong saw her first and nodded to her. Lena wished she could melt into the ground as Pastor turned and both men watched her come closer. She didn't have anywhere else to go, so she climbed up the steps and muttered an "excuse me." She entered the Building and turned to shut the door. Pastor and Mr. Armstrong were right behind her.

"We've talked with Mrs. Branson. Miss Ivory Bledsoe will be here in a few days, but she'll just be boarding in one of the rooms—that is, Mrs. Branson can spare an extra room for you."

Lena's jaw slacked in disbelief, but she kept her lips pressed tightly together as she looked around the Building. She knew Mrs. Branson owned it and rented rooms, but it was usually empty—a good sign that it was a fair price above everyone's income. "I'm not sure it's in my budget."

Mr. Armstrong gave her a smile. "She knows what you make."

"But I don't have this month's paycheck." Thanks to Mom.

"She knows," Pastor Stuart said gently.

"But I owe Mr. Clark." Or, Mom did. *Forgive.* It may be Mom's fault, but love covered a multitude of sins—even when it meant paying for a debt she didn't incur.

"I'll talk with Mr. Clark. Explain things."

Lena cringed. Pastor Stuart was well-meaning, but Mom had drilled into her that it was a crying shame to expose their family struggles to the public. But then, Pastor had reminded her that some burdens were meant to be borne by the church. And, if Mom wasn't here, Lena assumed it fell to the pastor to help take care of her problems. She took in a deep breath. "Thank you."

Mr. Armstrong slung an arm across Lena's shoulders and gave her a slow wink. "Don't worry, we'll take care of you."

Lena's throat tightened. *Like Mom never did.* All of the attention made her want to find a book and hide. She managed to keep still under Mr. Armstrong's brotherly hug and give him a ghost of a smile.

Mrs. Branson bustled into the room. "Room's ready." She raised her eyebrows at the small bundle Lena clutched. "Follow me."

It took just a few minutes for Lena to be situated in a room—her room—then Lena scrambled back to the library. It was closed for the evening, so she took out the key and let herself in. It went against protocol, but she needed this time alone, and she didn't think Mr. Armstrong would blame her. She went to the far side and sank down with her back against the shelf holding the history books. The events of the day whirled around in her brain. It was like Sara Crewe's eleventh birthday in *Little Princess*. Though Lena didn't go from a rich, pampered daughter to a maid overnight, the changes in her life were just as drastic and life-shattering.

She was out from under Mom's roof—but not at all like she had planned. Instead of feeling success at independence, fear threatened to weave its burrs into her heart. At the same time, a strange peace settled over her. She hadn't rebelled against Mom—Mom had left her. That last glimpse of Mom flashed through Lena's mind. For the first time, beneath the facade of grace and beauty, Lena saw something more than a woman who hated her. She saw a woman bound by bitterness and sadness—a woman who was reaping misery because of the indiscretion she had sown. And for the first time, Lena wished that Mom fully understood the love Jesus Christ had for her.

The library door creaked open and Lena instinctively stiffened.

"Lena?" It was Mrs. Stuart's soft voice.

She didn't try to hide, but stood up.

"Mrs. Branson said she thought she saw you slip in here."

"Yes ma'am." Lena took a step away from the bookcase.

"How are you doing?" Mrs. Stuart didn't envelope Lena in a hug like she had last night, but her kind smile warmed Lena's heart.

"I... I think everything will be fine."

As she said the words, she realized she meant it. She didn't know what exactly tomorrow held, but in just the last twenty-four hours, she'd seen proof of what Homer had assured her: God knew how to take care of her. Even if it was in ways totally unexpected.

"Come for supper?" Mrs. Stuart held out her hand to Lena.

She was too old to be catered to like a little girl, but Lena still slipped her fingers inside Mrs. Stuart's slender hand and allowed herself to be led away from the library. Like the Psalms said, God didn't let His children go hungry. Lena said a quick prayer of thanksgiving as she left the library behind her.

22

*L*ena crept out of her room and into the library. A thrill surged through her. She lived in the same building as the library. That was something she had never dreamed of. She grabbed the saddle bags that were packed and ready for today's route—Friday's route. And it wasn't her last route, thanks to Mr. Armstrong and Pastor Stuart. She had nearly forgotten about Aidan McGrew and his promise to get his clan interested in new books. But yesterday, she had picked out every single children's book she could. Some had a few more words to entice the children to learn some letters. And, if they allowed her, she'd settle down and teach them how to sound out the words. Today, anything felt possible.

Had it only been a week since she had seen that breakthrough on this route? It felt like a year had transpired. A stab of heaviness still threatened to dampen her eagerness as she walked to the stables. Mom hadn't given her any way to communicate. For all Lena knew, Mom could be planning to return and find a new way to make her life miserable. But that was borrowing tomorrow's trouble. After supper last night, Pastor Stuart had handed her a list of verses—full of hope and promises. She slid her fingertips into her jacket pocket, and they grazed the folded paper.

As soon as the sun illuminated the mountain, Lena slipped the paper out, giving Kirby his head while she read. She grinned at Pastor's scrawling handwriting, but the words and motive behind the poorly written words warmed her more than the rising sun ever could. He had talked through the verses with her and asked her to consider committing them to memory. She had promised she would—and starting right now, she'd hold true to that promise.

The first was Psalm 16:8-9. "I have set the LORD always before me: because He is at my right hand, I shall not be moved. Therefore my heart is glad, and my glory rejoiceth: my flesh also shall rest in hope."

Always keep God in your mind, Lena. That will keep you on the right path. Keep your heart full of praise. That will keep your heart resting in hope.

Psalm 71:14 was similar. "But I will hope continually, and will yet praise thee more and more."

Hope and praise must go hand-in-hand. As long as you worry, you will have a hard time keeping hold of hope.

And then he had scratched out the long passage of Psalm 37:3-8. "Trust in the LORD, and do good; so shalt thou dwell in the land, and verily thou shalt be fed. Delight thyself also in the LORD; and he shall give thee the desires of thine heart. Commit thy way unto the LORD; trust also in him; and he shall bring it to pass. And he shall bring forth thy righteousness as the light, and thy judgment as the noonday. Rest in the LORD, and wait patiently for him: fret not thyself because of him who prospereth in his way, because of the man who bringeth wicked devices to pass. Cease from anger, and forsake wrath: fret not thyself in any wise to do evil."

He just gave her a teasing grin and said he wasn't going to re-preach a message—and then he had summarized it. She guessed preachers had a hard time *not* preaching when something spoke to their hearts.

She started memorizing Psalm 71:14 as Kirby continued his journey up the mountain. "I will hope continually." There was such promise in those words. Such beauty. Such… love. Because she wasn't just hoping. She had to secure her hope in Jesus Christ and His book of promises for her.

"It's the book lady! She's come! She's here!"

Children spilled out from behind trees and rocks, and Kirby pranced nervously at the sudden noise as they surrounded him. "Shh, it's okay." Lena patted Kirby as a huge grin felt like it would split across her face.

"Let her git doon." Aidan pushed the children out of the way, and Lena dismounted.

Even as the children moved out the way, they chattered incessantly.

"We read all the books, ma'am."

"How many did ye bring this time?"

"Kin I look first?"

Aidan pushed them even further back. "Shush and let her speak. She's not going anywhere 'til we all hae a chance tae look." He looked up at her shyly. "At least, I hope not."

Lena pulled out a handful of books and held them out of the children's reach. "Nope, I'm not going anywhere today."

Sudden tears threatened to spill out. Not today, or next week, or the next. As the children eagerly crowded around her, she knew God would work everything out—just like He had worked it out here.

Epilogue

June 2, 1955

*L*ena stepped quietly down the hospital hall and through the metal double doors. The nurse had said it was in the next hallway—room 303. She had also given Lena a sympathetic smile.

It had been twelve years since Lena had last seen Mom. She knew the date well. It should have been a date marked with joy and excitement, but Mom had made sure it was marked with heartbreak and sorrow.

September 11, 1943. The second Saturday of the month. The day she and Jed Stuart had stood before witnesses to bind their lives together. Forever.

Lena stopped in front of room 303 and stared at the door as the memories flooded her.

"A preacher's boy? Girl, you ain't fit for him."

Lena closed her eyes. *Lord, I forgive her.* She had whispered the words so many times over the years. It had gotten easier with time, but today a new wave crashed.

"He ain't even as old as you. You're gonna henpeck him. I can just see it. Make his life miserable."

But it hadn't been miserable. Hard, yes. But watered with tears and nurtured with love and patience, their marriage was strong by the grace of God. And Lena was learning to move beyond the scars and hurt that hovered over her since childhood. She didn't want anything to hurt the three children God had blessed her and Jed with. She rested her hand on her growing stomach. Baby number four was soon on its way.

Jed's words from this morning echoed in her mind. *I'll be praying for you, Lena.*

Lena bowed her head and prayed, *Father, I need Your help. Your guidance. Your wisdom.* Then, she opened the door.

The room was dark and quiet. The gentle whirring of a machine and blinking lights were the only interruption. On the bed lay a woman. Her hair was gone. Her skin a pasty gray.

Lena took a step forward. Mom was only fifty-one. But she looked like she was almost seventy.

"Hi, Mom." She spoke softly, knowing Mom probably wouldn't respond. "Your friend Sandy found me." After all these years of praying and wondering and sometimes searching, it could only be explained as an answer to prayer that someone had taken the initiative to find Lena and inform her that Mom was in her last days of cancer.

Lena stopped at the chair by Mom's bedside. "I've been praying for you. Every day."

What more could she say? That she missed Mom? She wouldn't lie. Life had been easier when the wounds had a chance to heal rather than be reopened every week with fierce and heartless words.

"Jed and I have a family now. He's been so good to me." She sat in the chair and rested her hands on her lap. "You have three grandchildren. Joseph is seven, Rebekah is five, and David is two. There's another one coming soon." Lena usually smiled when she thought of this new blessing, but it didn't seem appropriate, not in this death-room. Not with the fresh realization that, just as Lena never knew her grandparents, her children would never know their grandmother. At least they had Jed's parents. Pastor Stuart and his wife spoiled their grandchildren, which warmed Lena's heart.

"Mom, I've forgiven you." Tears now stung Lena's eyes. She lowered her voice even more. "I forgive you."

How she had hoped and prayed the day would come when her relationship with Mom would be renewed—that they would be able to enjoy fellowship. Instead, Lena was speaking to an unconscious woman who was just a skeleton of the beauty and grace she had been decades before.

"I love you." Lena choked on the words. How many times had she yearned to hear the words from Mom? Now, she knew she never would. But that wouldn't change the love God had given her to bestow on Mom. "I want you to know that God loves you, too. He loves you so much, Mom." The tears now slipped down her cheeks. "I don't want to lose you for eternity. I know I wasn't a good daughter. I have regretted so much of what I said to you. But God's working in my heart, Mom. He's changed me so much because He loves me. And I know He loves you just as much as He loves me. He sent His Son, Jesus Christ, to die on the cross for your sins."

Mom had heard the Gospel plan many times in those days she sat in church with Lena, pretending to be an upright Christian woman. But she had never really listened. And now it may be too late.

"There is no sin greater than God's grace. Anything you did wrong, you can bring to the feet of Jesus and He'll wash and cleanse you from that sin. So then when you see Him…" Lena blinked back the tears and took a shuddering breath. "When you see Him, He can look at you through the blood of Jesus. And everything that you did wrong is forgiven in His eyes. But you *must* repent and accept Him as Savior."

Lena leaned forward and rested her hand on the white sheet beside Mom's thin, pale hand. She gently fingered Mom's knuckles. "I don't know if you can hear me, Mom, but please—*please* make things right with God before you die." She slipped her hand underneath Mom's and gently squeezed it. She leaned her head against the rail of the hospital bed and squeezed her eyes shut. She couldn't say anything more. Her heart was crying a prayer that could never be uttered through words.

After a long while, she looked back up at Mom. "I do forgive you, Mom. And I do love you." She knew she meant it, now that she was seeing Mom face to face.

Mom's face remained blank. The machine continued whirring. The lights steadily blinked.

Ever so subtly, Mom's fingers tightened around Lena's.

Historical Note

$\mathcal{L}$ena's story could have really happened.

Kentucky was one of the worst-hit states during the Great Depression. Its main source of income—coal mining—had plummeted, leaving families all over the mountainside without employment. Even though the United States had progressed in technology by the 1930s, many in the Appalachians had no running water, electricity, or, in some places, schools.

While President Roosevelt began his Works Progress Administration (WPA) as part of his New Deal, his wife, Eleanor, advocated the Packhorse Librarian Program. Not only would it help educate the illiterate Kentuckians, but it would also provide income for many women (and a few men) in Kentucky counties.

These librarians were usually locals. They would get up as early as 4:30 to care for their own families before heading out to ride a route as long as eighteen miles. Traveling through all kinds of weather was only half the battle. They also had to earn the trust of those they were hoping to serve.

To prove they were trustworthy, some librarians would quote the Bible. Each librarian had her own route that she rode at least twice monthly, covering 100-120 miles. She would make $28 a month (equivalent to $495 in modern money), paid for by the WPA.

Since most counties were poor, they relied on donations from others around the nation. Some book donations came from as far as California. Not all of the books donated were usable, though, and librarians spent hours mending books or repurposing magazines into original scrapbooks. By 1940, over 2,500 scrapbooks were created, filled with recipes, history, dogs, mountain ballads, odd names, and more.

The Packhorse Librarian Program ended in 1943, as World War II eased the effects of the Great Depression. It is estimated that almost 1,000 horseback librarians were employed during the program and twenty-nine counties were served. Many say the Packhorse Librarian Program was only the start as mobile libraries have continued to bring books to less populated areas.

Author's Note

*I*n many ways, "A Strand of Hope" deals with harder topics than I have previously dealt with in my fiction writing. Unlike Lena, I was super blessed to have been raised in a godly home with both parents. But I know many, many Christian young people who did not have that blessing. While some use it as an excuse for why they can't follow God, I admire those in my life who have been shining examples of following God, even when those closest to them made it difficult.

Having Nora's dementia woven into Lena's story was a good way to show a picture of Homer's unconditional love, but it is also a cameo of my own life. For the past few years, I have watched as dementia has affected my grandmother and has completely changed her from the person she was. It is challenging to watch those we love change, and as I edited Nora's parts of the story, tears came to my eyes. I wish I didn't know how to portray a dementia patient, but sometimes God allows us to go through these hard steps of life to give us practical ways to share His love with others. If you have a loved one struggling with dementia or Alzheimer's, don't stop loving them when they change. You never know how your love to them will be observed by someone else and impact their lives.

The messages Lena lives in this story are ones that are close to my own heart. Choosing to forgive and not to let bitterness rule in our hearts is a choice we have to make often as Christians. Even if we learn the lesson with one person, we can be guaranteed there will be another opportunity to exercise forgiveness and love to another person when it feels like the last thing we want to do. "And let us not be weary in well doing…" (Galatians 6:9)

J am thankful for the life God has given me and for the lessons He has taught me. They so often end up on the pages of my stories. I want to live a life so that no trial is wasted because I didn't learn from it. So yes, I'm even thankful for the trials and my God Who is faithful through them all!

I am thankful for my family who has shown me a picture of unconditional love. My parents, siblings, siblings-in-law, nieces, and nephews have added so much richness to my life.

I am thankful for a plethora of friends who have helped me in my writing journey:

Kenzi—you stepped in when my health was faltering and offered to combine my alpha reader notes so I had one less step to do in editing. And you also spent part of your visit doing final proofreading so I could meet deadlines. That means the world to me.

Faith, Anita, and Alicia—you are my Horseback pals. Wow, what an experience this has been! As my first time doing a joint-author project, it has been a very good experience. You all were so patient with me as I went MIA with college work and had to re-ask questions that you were all settled on. Lena's story wouldn't be nearly as exciting if it didn't have Lillian's, Ivory's, and Edna's following close on its heels.

Bro. Josh Lang—for allowing me to steal your sermon notes to use for Pastor Stuart's message.

My alpha readers—A.M. Heath, Faith Blum, Alicia Ruggieri, Emily Hebert, and Kenzi Knapp; I always hesitate to hand out my roughest draft to readers, but you all plowed through and gave me sound advice that made it much more solid of a story.

My beta readers—Michaela Bush, Kaitlyn Smith, Annalissa Labonte, Jordy Leigh, Erika Mathews, Evangeline Gaharan, Mary Polakvo, Patti Pierce, Faith Gilliosa, Ryana Lynn, LeAnne, Lauren Compton, Kate Thompson, Janell Rogers, and Malina Mangrum. You are awesome! I had so many typos and weird phrases you caught, and it wasn't even your responsibility to do so! You went above and beyond, and I'm super grateful! Added to that, some of you sent me the most encouraging and uplifting emails. Hearing first-hand that you love Lena's story was the boost I needed!

My launch team—Wendy Heuvel, Roger Lowther, Abigail, Kim Hampton, Olivia Rooney, Michaela Bush, Emily Kopf, Stephanie Daniels, Becky Dempsey, Kelly-Ann Deffenbaugh, Anne Wolffe, Kylie Hunt, Tarissa Graves, Melanie Kurz, Jeniver Boyer, Amanda Buhler, Jana Tenbrook, Jordy Leigh, Joshua Reid, Connie, Ryana Miller, Kaitlyn Smith, Malina Mangrum, Kaitlyn Krispense, Tara Herring, Sarah Steele, Kassie Angle, Kenzi Knapp, Hannah Leake, Susan Brehmer, Ora Smith, Lana Christian, Emily Pugh, and Rebekah Morris. You got "A Strand of Hope" into more hands—so thank you, thank you, thank you!

My readers—if you have read this far, *thank you!* Unless you're an author yourself, you just will not understand the depth of gratitude I have for each and every reader. Thank you for letting my little story grace your shelves (or take up a few bytes on your e -reader).

Amanda Tero

About Amanda

Amanda Tero went straight from phonetics to scribbling before she understood spelling. Though none of her one-inch letters will ever be published, she has since grown up and introduced the world to her faith-filled novellas: A Strand of Hope, Journey to Love, and the Tales of Faith series. She's a picky bibliophile on a quest to fill bookshelves with pages of clean, accurate, and edifying stories, specifically for the YA Christian reader.

Her childhood as one of twelve kids in a preacher's home gave her many lessons on Biblical forgiveness, endurance, friendship, and love. She weaves this knowledge into the lives of characters who take the daring, difficult, and daunting paths, leaving readers with a glimpse of how to apply Scriptural teachings in realistic ways. When she's not surrounded by words, Amanda educates students in understanding a different alphabet on piano and violin.

Connect Online

Website: www.amandatero.com
Email: amanda@amandatero.com
Facebook: www.facebook.com/amandateroauthor
Instagram: @amandateroauthor
Twitter: @amandaterobooks
Pinterest: pinterest.com/amandateroauthor
Goodreads: AmandaTero
Amazon: amazon.com/author/amandatero

Get a free short story by signing up to my newsletter:

amandatero.com/newsletter

Help Me Out

Can you spend just two minutes to help me out?

Unlike the stereotype, being an author is *not* a solo act! Not only do I need the awesome behind-the-scenes staff... I also need *your* help!

A very simple and quick way to help is by leaving a review. Reviews are worth way more than their weight in chocolate (or gold, if you prefer to think that way).

Go to where you bought this book and leave just a ten-word review (or more, if you're wordy like me). It can be as simple as mentioning one thing you liked about the book.

Reviews not only help me be able to write more books, they also help other readers know that—hey, there's a book out there they might want to read! It's a win-win situation and *you* can help make it happen!

A.M. Heath

Hearts on Lonely Mountain

***Can two lonely people find more
than a fleeting friendship or will
a prejudiced town keep them apart?***

When Ivory Bledsoe left the city to
minister to the people of the rural
mountain town of Willow Hollow, she
never expected to be shunned rather
than welcomed. Seeing the town
as a lost cause, she's eager to return
home, but when the bridge leading out
of own is washed away during a flood, she finds
herself stranded in the last place she wants to be.

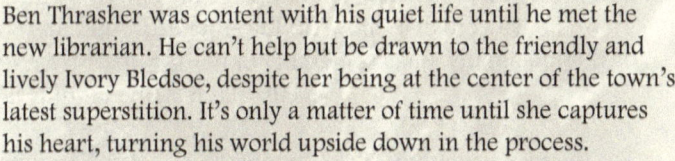

Ben Thrasher was content with his quiet life until he met the
new librarian. He can't help but be drawn to the friendly and
lively Ivory Bledsoe, despite her being at the center of the town's
latest superstition. It's only a matter of time until she captures
his heart, turning his world upside down in the process.

Has Ivory gotten God's plan for her all wrong or is there still a
way she can serve these people? And can Ben ask her to stay in
a place where so few are willing to embrace her?

christianauthoramheath.net

Alicia G. Ruggieri

The Secret Place of Thunder

***The mountains have imprisoned
her long enough...***

Edna Sue O'Connell came back to the
Kentucky hills out of duty and can't
wait for the chance to escape again.
Her work as a horseback librarian in
rural Appalachia provides enough
income for her invalid father to
survive in the midst of the Great
Depression, but it affords her with little else.

When an opportunity arises for Edna to take on an additional
book delivery area, she spies a glimmer of hope that she might
find a way out of Willow Hollow after all... and that she
might actually make something of her life apart from the
tragedy that has filled it thus far.

But the new routes give Edna more than she ever bargained
for. Slowly, she finds that the mountains contain many
valuable secrets – if she has the grit to meet them.

aliciagruggieri.com

More from Amanda

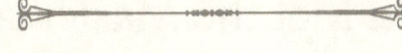

Short Stories

Novellas

Tales of Faith trilogy

Have you Met the Master Author?

The "author and finisher of our faith," the "author of salvation?"

Well, why do we need to know the Master Author?

There is no man, woman, boy, or girl who is without sin. Romans 3:23 says, "For **all** have sinned, and come short of the glory of God;"

Have you lied, cheated, stolen, taken God's Name in vain, coveted, or lusted? All of these are sins according to God's Holy law (see Exodus 20).

Even if we neglect in just one area of God's law, we are found sinners. "For whosoever shall keep the whole law, and yet offend in one point, he is guilty of all." (James 2:10) The payment for sin is death ("For the wages of sin is death;" Romans 6:23a)

God does not desire to leave us in this hopeless, destitute state. He did what we could not do and paid the debt for us.

He sent His Son, Jesus Christ, to come, be born of a virgin, live a sinless, perfect life, die a cruel death, and rise again, victorious over sin, death, and hell! Romans 6:23 continues to say, "but the gift of God is eternal life through Jesus Christ our Lord." Jesus Christ is the only way to have eternal life, to be forgiven ("Jesus saith unto him, I am the way, the truth, and the life: no man cometh unto the Father, but by me." John 14:6). God promised us that, "If we confess our sins, He is faithful and just to forgive us our sins, and to cleanse us from all unrighteousness." (1 John 1:9)

Salvation comes by putting your faith and trust in Jesus Christ for salvation and eternity ("Believe on the Lord Jesus Christ, and thou shalt be saved," Acts 16:31) and repenting from our sins ("Repent ye therefore, and be converted, that your sins may be blotted out," Acts 3:19).

So, have you met the Author?

www.ingramcontent.com/pod-product-compliance
Lightning Source LLC
Chambersburg PA
CBHW020911180626
46816CB00007BA/2343

* 9 7 8 1 9 4 2 9 3 1 3 2 4 *